THE DARK HORSE

Other books by Marcus Sedgwick

FLOODLAND

WITCH HILL

THE DARK HORSE

Marcus Sedgwick

with illustrations by the author

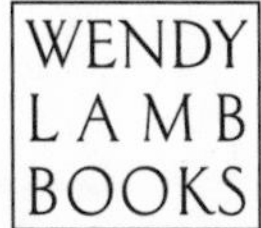

Published by
Wendy Lamb Books
an imprint of
Random House Children's Books
a division of Random House, Inc.
1540 Broadway
New York, New York 10036

Visit us on the Web! www.randomhouse.com/kids
Educators and librarians, for a variety of teaching tools, visit us at www.randomhouse.com/teachers

Library of Congress Cataloging-in-Publication Data

Sedgwick, Marcus.
The Dark Horse / Marcus Sedgwick.
p. cm.
Summary: Having risen to power as chief of his people, the Storn, sixteen-year-old Sigurd leads them as they try to resist the bloodthirsty invaders known as the Dark Horse and makes a shocking discovery about his foster sister Mouse.
ISBN 0-385-73054-3 (trade)—ISBN 0-385-90091-0 (lib. bdg.)
[1. Human-animal communication—Fiction. 2. Adventure and adventurers—Fiction.] I. Title.
PZ7.S4484 Dar 2003
[Fic]—dc21

2002005655

The text of this book is set in 12.5-point Opti Forquet Oldstyle and 13-point Mercurius Light.

Printed in the United States of America

February 2003

10 9 8 7 6 5 4 3 2

BVG

For my mother

Part One

THE BOX

1

It was Mouse who found the box. She was trotting along the tide line, running with Sigurd. Looking for sea cabbage washed up in the black sand after last night's storm, because the fishing had been bad again. They were half a day from home.

Flicking the hair from her eyes, Mouse tilted her head to one side.

"Sigurd?"

Sigurd came over to where Mouse stood. He towered above her.

"What is it, Mouse?"

"That."

She nodded at the box. It was different. It didn't belong here. All around them was the coast—rocky outcrops, with the low hills behind—and the sea, the sea, the sea in front of them. Everything was the wildness of Storn. And amongst all this wildness lay the box. A small wooden box—a couple of hands wide but quite slender. There was no metal visible—no hinges or corner braces. No lock. It was a plain wooden box, but somehow it was very beautiful. It was made of a deep and rich red wood, black in places. It had a shine that reflected the light from the sky back onto Mouse's small, round face.

It *was* different. It was from somewhere else.

Mouse felt her head swim a little. She staggered a few paces away from the box.

"Mouse?" Sigurd had noticed. "Anything?"

Sigurd was used to spotting the signs, better than anyone else at knowing when Mouse might "see" something. But she put her hand on Sigurd's arm.

"No," she said. "No, it's gone now."

Mouse drew in a deep, calming breath. They turned their attention back to the box, but Mouse kept her distance. "What do you think it is?"

Sigurd said nothing. He knelt down to touch it, but gently, as if it were a cornered animal.

"It's dry," he said. "It's . . . warm."

"What is it?" Mouse asked again.

"Shall I open it?"

Mouse shook her head.

"Let's take it back."

Mouse hesitated.

"It's getting late," he reasoned.

"All right," she said.

They started back to the village, Sigurd carrying the box, Mouse with a net half full of cabbage.

Neither of them had noticed the man lying still amongst the rocks, just twenty paces from where they had found the box. His skin and hair were white, whiter even than Sigurd's, but the palms of his hands were black.

2

I remember better than anyone.

I remember better than anyone the day we found Mouse.

It was unusual that we should have been up in the hills in the first place. There were about thirty of us, I think. A huge war party—going to wage war on . . . wolves.

Father said it was stupid. Just because a lone wolf had attacked Snorri as he came home over the hills was no reason to risk our lives. That's what my father said, though he didn't say it to Horn's face.

As I remember, it was only a couple of summers after Horn had beaten Father for the title of Lawspeaker of the tribe. Father was licking his wounds then, I suppose. He swore that one day he'd tell Horn to his face what he thought of him, but not then.

That probably had something to do with it. The fight, I mean. Why we were up in the hills, hunting wolves. That was stupid, too. Wolves live in woods, and there were no trees up there. Horn was showing us all that he was our leader, that we had to do whatever he told us.

I was the only child there, and I *was* a child then. It was my eleventh or twelfth summer; I can't remember. I was a part of the games Horn and Father played.

"Well, Sigurd," Father said to me, "if that fool is going to take us on a wild wolf chase, we may as well show him what kind of family we are!"

What this meant was that he'd take the opportunity to show me, his son, off to everyone. Because Horn, the Lawspeaker, had no son, only a daughter, Sif. There was no one to succeed him as Lawspeaker, and so there would have to be a fight for the job, just as there had been between him and Olaf, my father.

It was late in the day when we reached the higher slopes of the hills. A couple of the hounds had picked up the scent of something hours ago, and we'd been following the trail ever since. Once or twice they'd lost the scent and we'd hung around while Hemm, a small, clever man who was our best dog handler, made wide circles around us with his hound. Eventually the dog would find a scent and we'd be off again, always higher up into the hills.

"If that's still the scent of the wolves," muttered Father, loud enough for only me to hear, "I'll wash Horn's feet before bedtime."

On we went, higher and higher, until suddenly we came to the top of a slope, and there in front of us, no more than a spear's throw away, were the small, dark entrances to a series of caves. The dogs were going crazy, pulling toward them, and suddenly the mood changed. I felt a touch of fear stroke me.

There was a chill in the air. We were high above the sea, directly above the village, though you couldn't see it from there. There really were wolves here, and they had chosen somewhere special to live. I had never heard of wolves living in caves. Forests are their usual home. And I have never heard of another case since. We should have realized then that it was an omen.

It hadn't seemed real until that moment, but now Horn's ridiculous wolf chase was actually happening. It had actually come to something. We avoided one another's gaze; no one looked at Horn.

But he stepped forward, undaunted. He wasn't about to turn around and go home.

"This is what we've come for," he said quietly.

"So what do we do?"

"You want us to go in there?"

"They'll rip us to pieces before we even see them. . . ."

Horn held up his hand.

"Let's lighten their darkness. Let's get them out here." He pointed at Grinling. "Grinling! Make fire."

So then we understood what he meant to do.

3

After they found the box, it took Mouse and Sigurd more than three hours to get home. They were tired and spoke little as they went. They walked up from the shore to the brochs of the village while the sun began to sink into the sea horizon out in the bay.

Storn, the village, was just a cluster of these brochs—mostly round stone houses with turf roofs that each family lived in, maybe thirty or so in all. The grass of the turf roofs made the houses blend in with the grass and ferns that grew all around the settlement. It seemed as if the brochs grew from the landscape, rather than being built upon it. The edge of the village was marked by no boundary, no fence, not even a ditch, but just ran off into grassland and the fields behind, and the pebbles and black sand of the beach in front.

More or less in the middle was the great broch—a large meeting hall that dominated the village. It was nearly twice the height of the rest of the brochs.

There were other buildings, too. Mouse and Sigurd picked their way carefully past the grain barns and smoke-houses, the kennels and the goat huts. They were both exhausted. There didn't seem to be anyone else around. They could see orange flames from the fire in the great broch through its low, round doorway. They paused. Only now did they consider the box.

"Where shall we take it?" asked Mouse.

"What do you think's in it?" asked Sigurd, grinning. "I bet it's treasure!"

He thought it must have come from one of the trading ships that sailed up to them from far away in the south. In a way he was right.

"Let's open it!" he said.

Mouse said nothing. Something worried her, but she did not understand what it was.

Before they could decide what to do, a huge figure blocked the firelight coming from the great broch and strode toward them.

"Sigurd! Come here, boy!"

It was Olaf, and he was cross. He pushed his rough hand through his beard. That meant he was nervous, too.

"We've been waiting for our cabbage! And the Spell-making is about to start!"

"Coming, Father!" called Sigurd.

They hurried to the broch, but Mouse stumbled, catching her feet in the cabbage net. Olaf put out a huge hand and caught her and the net together.

"Is this all?" he asked, looking from the half-empty net to Sigurd.

Sigurd started to burn with humiliation, but Mouse spoke.

"Yes," she said simply.

Olaf's face softened a little.

"The sea is abandoning us, eh, Mouse? No fish today, either. Go inside, it's nearly time."

They went in. Olaf gave his son a clip round the head as he passed, but it was gentler than it might have been.

"He thinks I'm useless," Sigurd said to Mouse.

"That's not true. He loves you."

"Why's he always so hard on *me*? He's supposed to be *your* father, too."

As soon as he said this, Sigurd regretted it.

Mouse looked at him. "But he isn't, is he."

They wove their way through the villagers gathered in the great broch. Trying to find a quiet spot to sit in for the Spell-making, trying to sit as far away as possible from Sif, Horn's daughter. From experience they found it best to avoid her. When they saw her right across the other side of the fire from them, they sat down, at the edge, by the wall. This was where Mouse preferred to sit, and not just because of Sif.

Sigurd knew why but never spoke to Mouse about it. He knew she was still a little wary of fire.

The Spell-making was about to begin, as it had done at every quarter of the moon since anyone could remember.

It was only then that Mouse remembered.

"The box!" she whispered. "What have you done with the box?"

Sigurd smiled.

"I'm cleverer than some people think!"

But now Gudrun, the Wisewoman, was entering the circle, where she joined Horn, the Lawspeaker. The Spell-making began.

Mouse was silent.

Away, far down the sea line, the white man with black hands lay amongst the rocks in the darkness. He lay still. But the tide was returning, and as the first slush of salty foam washed across his face, he stirred. Immediately, even before his eyes had opened, his hands searched for something. Something that was missing.

4

What a mess!

Grinling striking his flint without success. Horn stamping around the place.

"Hasn't anyone got any dry tinder?" Horn barked.

No one spoke.

"Wait, boy," my father whispered to me, "wait until he's really seething."

A dangerous game, but Father wanted to make the most of any chance to get at Horn.

Finally Horn lost his patience and kicked Grinling hard in the backside.

"Go on, then," said Father through his teeth. "Now."

I stepped forward, a huge rock in my belly. That was fear. I was scared of Horn.

"Please, Lawspeaker," I said. "Please, is this any use?"

I tried to sound innocent of Olaf's game, but I think Horn

knew what was going on. He stared at the mugwort in my hand. Dry, fluffy, and perfect for catching sparks with.

"Is this any use?" I said again. I wasn't really asking. We both knew it *was*.

If Horn knew the game we were playing, he didn't show it. But with everyone staring at him, he couldn't appear to be bested by a boy. A boy of no more than twelve summers.

He grunted and waved a paw at Grinling.

"Let this boy show you how," he said, shifting the shame onto Grinling.

So I lit the torches, which we carried to the mouths of the wolves' caves, while Father was congratulated for having such a clever son.

"Olaf, you must be so proud!"

And did they say it within Horn's earshot?

No, not then.

Who was it?

I can't think now. How terrible not to remember who it was whose throat was ripped out by a wolf's fangs.

Oh. It was Snorri.

It was as if fate were dealing the blows, because it was in retaliation for the attack on Snorri that Horn had dragged us up into the hills anyway.

Grinling threw a torch into the darkness of the first cave.

Then, holding another flare in front of him, Snorri stuck his head into the cave.

Behind him the sun was starting to set on the sea horizon,

flooding the sky with the color of the blood that was about to spill across the rocks around the cave mouth.

Snorri's head was followed out of the cave by a surge of fur and claw that raged from the darkness within.

The wolves poured out. It's my belief they had smelt us a long while before, and were waiting and brooding in their home. We had lit a match and started a fire.

So they poured out and away down the hill, and two more of us were dead before the sun had sunk another hairsbreadth.

And no, I am afraid I cannot remember who they were.

Then, despite the screaming and the shouting, all noise ceased. At least, it did in my head, for my eyes fell to the front of the cave, where there stood a girl.

A small girl, naked and dirty, standing quietly in a frame of shadow, with a look on her face . . . of confusion.

Mouse.

5

Smoke curled thickly from the fire pit and twisted around inside the darkness of the broch until it found its way eventually out of the small hole in the roof of the round house. Somewhere in a dark corner the hounds snored. The Storn sat in small groups, waiting for the Spell-making to begin. Another hard day had ended, and the ceremony at least gave them a break from the usual routine. Everyone was still and quiet. The fire threw a red light onto their faces. They were faces that had been shaped by the wind and the salt and the rain that came with living on the coast.

In the center of the broch, next to the fire, sat Horn. His own face was deeply lined, worn by the weather and by leadership. It was as rough as the rocks that the broch was built from. At more than forty years, he was amongst the older of the Storn, though nearby sat Longshank, who was the oldest.

Longshank was the Lawkeeper. He had learned all the history of the tribe, told to him as a young man by the previous Lawkeeper. He was often called on to advise on difficult and serious matters, though he had no power himself. All the power lay with the Lawspeaker.

With Horn by the fire sat Gudrun, the Wisewoman. She was more than thirty years old and had never taken a husband. She was large, and might have seemed fat but for her height. Long brown hair and the hood of her thick deerskin cloak hid her face. She began to make the spells to keep the Storn safe, to bring them food, to bring them whatever they needed or wanted.

"Bring us fish, make us warm, lift the sun, stop the snow, sharpen our tools, heat our fires, forge our iron, grow our grain, still the wind. . . ."

Her voice began its hourlong journey through their fears and desires.

The faces in the great broch watched intently. Though they had seen it all many times before, they needed the Spellmaking, believing fiercely in its power to protect them.

But at the back of the hall Mouse and Sigurd were thinking about something else.

"We shouldn't have brought it here," Mouse said, whispering quietly to Sigurd, her head bowed.

"You mean Sif? She won't notice, she's too busy painting her skin these days to—anyway, it's far too cold outside and there's nowhere—"

"No, Siggy. I mean we shouldn't have brought it, touched it at all."

Gudrun's voice continued to spell out her magic. "Bring the herds, brew our beer, strengthen our babies. . . ."

Sigurd sneaked a look at Mouse's face, trying to get at what she meant.

"All finds are Horn's property, that's his right as Lawspeaker."

"No, Siggy, I don't mean that, either. I'm not scared of Horn—"

"And nor am I," Sigurd whispered back.

"I'm scared of the box, Sigurd. The box."

Now Sigurd understood. "You felt something? At the beach?"

Mouse shrugged.

"I wasn't sure," she said defensively, "you know what I'm like... sometimes it's not clear. There might just have been some animal nearby... I might have been feeling its fear of us instead...."

She stopped, sensing something else entirely now. Although she hadn't lifted her head, she knew Sigurd wasn't listening to her anymore.

She looked up. Horn stood in front of her. Gudrun was still speaking, down in the center, by the fire, but as Horn held up his hand she stopped.

The entire community of Storn was staring at Mouse.

"Well, girl, what is it? What is it that is more important to you and Olaf the Weakling's son than the Spell-making?"

Horn spoke quietly, his voice only just audible over the crackle of the fire, but there was an edge to it that made it clear.

Mouse trembled.

"I'm sorry, Horn. We were talking of the poor fishing and the poor finds to be had on the shore. That's all. I'm sorry."

"You. Olaf's boy," said Horn to Sigurd, though he was still staring at Mouse, "what do you say?"

"That's all, Horn, just the poor finds along the beach. And the fishing—"

"They're lying!"

Sif. Horn's daughter.

Mouse shuddered, fearful of what Sif would do.

Horn turned and strode to the center of the circle. As he stood by the fire the flames lit his face with an orange glow. He looked terrifying.

"Well?" he said, staring at his daughter.

Sif stood up, a little nervously. She hid behind her long black hair. Nevertheless, Mouse could see one of her slate gray eyes fixed right on her.

Sif knew she was risking embarrassing her father, but she wasn't going to miss the chance to humiliate Sigurd and Mouse. She disliked them, maybe even hated them. She hated their closeness.

As she looked at them now, standing next to each other, practically clinging to each other for comfort, the envy rose in her again.

"Father . . . ," she began, then remembered where they were. "Lawspeaker . . . they found something on the beach. I saw them."

"Go on," said Horn. Something in his voice indicated he was scared his daughter might embarrass him if she was not careful.

"They hid it. Sigurd hid it from his own father. *She* pretended to fall, and he hid it outside the broch."

"What was it? Food?"

A muttering rose from those gathered at the assembly. Sigurd looked toward his parents. Freya, his mother, tried to smile at her son, but then Olaf caught his eye. His father's face raged with a mixture of shame and anger.

"No," said Sif, "it was this."

She turned and knelt down. From underneath the blanket she'd been sitting on she produced the box.

She held it up for everyone to see, and there was silence.

6

Of course, she wasn't called Mouse then.

When we found her, four summers before *she* found the box, she wasn't called anything. She was just a girl we found in a cave full of wolves.

After a while others noticed what I was looking at. They turned and saw the naked girl, standing in the cave mouth. Still she did not move. Her hair was long and unkempt. She was filthy. She was perhaps seven or eight summers old, but it was hard to tell.

"What's this?" asked my father. He came and stood by my side.

"Look!" I said. "She's crying!"

"Poor thing," said Selva, one of the few women who'd come with us on the war party.

"It's a miracle she's still alive," said someone else.

There was confusion. Still the girl stood staring at us, crying quietly. And then I remember very clearly, though I don't remember who said it:

"How could a little mouse like that have survived in there? With those animals?"

A little mouse.

"They must have been saving her. You know, to eat later."

A little mouse. I can't remember much after that. How we took her home to the village. There was a lot of debate, that I do remember. Argument while we were still on the hill.

It was obvious we had to take her. Obvious to everyone apart from Horn, that is.

"Another mouth to feed, that's all she is," he said.

"But we can't just leave her!" I cried.

Olaf put his hand over my mouth, but Horn hadn't even heard me.

"You don't have to worry about feeding her," he said, "I do. I have to see you're all fed. . . ."

No one spoke for a while. There was a standoff. Then Father stepped forward.

"What's the matter, Lawspeaker?" he said. "Is it beyond your powers to feed a tiny girl like this?"

Horn must have sensed that the mood was against him, because though he spat on the ground at my father's feet, he gave in.

"Very well. But the child will belong to your family, Olaf. It will be on your head."

And I do also remember that though we had decided the girl was coming with us, the girl herself had not.

She had not spoken a word, and then she struggled and fought.

"She's out of her mind."

"She's just scared."

"Who knows how long she's been here!"

But she came with us in the end. The caves were empty, the wolves had gone. It was time to get down off the hill. Before we got home, we had stopped calling her the mouse and just called her Mouse instead.

That was that.

We put a cloak around her and left the hill.

About halfway down the stillness of the evening air was suddenly broken. There was a cry from a wolf high above us. A single long, piercing howl that stopped us in our tracks. It was a sad sound, it seemed to me.

I looked at Mouse, to see her reaction, but she was still crying. Crying tears of relief, I assumed. But then she held back her tears, sucked in a huge breath, and let out a long, heartbreaking wolf howl.

We looked at one another, hesitating for a moment, and then we set off again down the hill, a little faster than before.

Olaf, my father, carried Mouse all the way back to the village on his back.

I was so proud. And not just of my father, for some reason.

No one knew then what Mouse was. What she could *do*.

Horn thought he was giving us an extra mouth to feed and nothing more, but he was wrong.

We began to understand when we found her sleeping with the hounds.

But wait—I am telling this the wrong way round.

It was hard at first for Mouse.

Weeks went by. She hadn't spoken a single word. We thought she was mute. We had cleaned her up. Washed and cut her hair. Found that there was a girl underneath all the dirt, though a strange-looking girl she was. She was small and delicate; she had a small, round, delicate face, with huge and beautiful eyes. She tried to hide behind the hair we had left straggling down in front of her face.

She didn't seem to know where she was at first. What she was doing with us. Though she hadn't spoken, she seemed to understand what we told her. Food, sleep, things like that.

She would nod her head, or tip it to one side if she wasn't sure.

But if anyone tried, and they *did* try, to ask her anything more complicated, she would just stare blankly through them.

"When did the wolves capture you, Mouse?" asked Freya, my mother.

"What's your name?" asked Olaf, my father.

"Where are you from? Really?" I asked.

Any of these questions brought the same response from Mouse. She would stare through you as if she were looking at something in the distance.

We decided she was simple. Stupid. Perhaps as a result of being caught by those wolves, we thought. Perhaps it had scared her out of her mind.

And then one day we lost her.

She'd been kept in our own broch since we found her. If she went outside, it was with my mother, and only for a short time. She had nothing to do; we'd given her no work, and she would just sit in the darkness of the broch, blinking from time to time. Outside she seemed even more timid.

"She likes the darkness," my mother said to my father.

He nodded.

"Like the cave," he said. "Now, why should that be?"

So we'd grown used to her sitting in the darkest corner of our dark little broch, saying nothing, taking food when offered, sleeping when we did.

But then, as I say, we lost her.

My mother said she thought she was still in the broch, but when Father and I came back from fishing, we saw she was not there.

"But I never saw her leave!" Mother cried. "She was here!"

We searched all over the village, trying not to attract attention. But it was a busy time of day, with men coming back from fishing and pulling the boats up the beach, and women returning from the fields.

"Lost something, Olaf?" Herda, the Song-giver, asked my father.

He held up his hand as if to say, "Be quiet," but it was too late.

So Herda and a few others joined the search, and Mouse was found. Sleeping with the hounds in the farthest darkness of the great broch.

A crowd had gathered as Father pulled Mouse blinking into the light.

Horn was standing by, a mocking smile on his face.

"Your daughter prefers the company of dogs?" he said.

There was laughter. Not kind laughter.

My father was embarrassed. He shook Mouse angrily by the shoulder. It was one of the few times I saw him angry with her.

"What are you thinking of?" he shouted. "Lying with dogs!"

Then, and then, and then! Mouse spoke for the first time!

"But they were sad," she said.

For a while we were all too amazed that she'd spoken at all, never mind what she had said. Never mind the strange accent to her voice.

Olaf gathered himself.

"What did you say?" he asked her.

"The dogs are sad since Graylegs died," Mouse said simply, as if it were obvious. Graylegs was one of the older hounds. He had died a couple of days before.

"What? How do you know they're sad?" Father asked, bewildered.

"They told me," said Mouse.

Then she asked her first question. That look of confusion she'd had on her face when we first saw her had returned.

"Why?" she asked. "Don't they talk to you?"

7

In front of a small fire, in a shelter of branches and bracken, the man with white hair and skin rubbed the black palms of his hands together. He felt warm enough, but he shivered, as if with a fever. He spread all his possessions out before him by the jumping firelight.

First. His knife, the length of a hand, with a different blade on each side, one toothed and one smooth. As good for skinning a goat as cutting a throat.

Second. Some leather cord, for various purposes.

Third. A little dried fish.

Fourth. An oiled bag containing his fire sticks.

Fifth was the leather bag in which he carried these things. That was all. His only other possessions were his clothes and a charm around his neck, a round metal disc with a picture of a horse on it. How he wished he still had his horse for this task... but she had died when he was only a year into his journey.

He'd been heading north when the ship ran aground on the reef in the storm. It had irritated him to learn that he'd already passed the place, had gone too far south. He'd had to find a ship heading back the way he'd come.

None of the traders whose ship it was seemed to have survived the shipwreck. It hadn't been far to the shore, but they'd all been drunk. He'd despised them for it as he clung desperately to the box with one arm and swam inland with the other, the cord of his leather bag tightening around his neck with every stroke.

So he'd go on going north. It was always possible the box had been washed out to sea while he lay unconscious on the beach, but he didn't think so. He'd seen footsteps near him in the sand, though the tide had washed most of them away, and there was no trail to follow. Besides, he'd come too far to fail. He had to succeed. And he had to have the box to do it.

Without it he felt anxious. It was his reason for being here; in a way it was simply his reason for being. After years of traveling, and so close to the end of his journey, he'd lost it.

He held the charm in his hand and vowed he would find the box. It was too cold to sleep tonight, but before the sun had set on him tomorrow, he *would* find the box. He shivered again, and a drop of sweat fell from his forehead into his eye. He ignored it, his mind on more important things.

No one else knew what the box held, and even if they did, he was safe enough for now. The box had its own protection.

8

After Sif had produced the box, Horn had shouted at Mouse and Sigurd. And after Horn had shouted at them, Olaf had shouted at them, in front of everyone. After that people had begun to be more interested in the box itself, and Mouse and Sigurd had fled the great broch, Sif laughing at them, and Freya chasing after Sigurd, trying to console him.

Mouse had no idea where Sigurd was now. It seemed he didn't want even her around. But it wasn't just his fault that Sif had seen him hide the box. They'd been careless. Mouse wondered what was in the box. Horn would find out now and keep whatever treasures were inside it.

Mouse had crept into one of the small brochs used as a grain store. She'd put her blanket up onto the pile of wheat and gone to sleep. She'd done it before. It was a place she came to whenever she needed to hide. She wasn't allowed to sleep with the dogs, so she came here. Not even Siggy knew. If she heard anyone coming, she'd learned how to wriggle down into the grain and hide, and if a few last ears of wheat spilled onto the floor as whoever it was opened the door, they'd say, "Just a mouse," not knowing how right they were.

The last time Mouse had hidden in the grain, not that long ago, she'd had to throw her blanket onto the top of the pile, and herself after it. This time she'd only had to step up onto it. They were using up their stores of wheat. The fishing was very bad, and it was a long time till Harvest-month. Olaf had dared to mention this at a gathering in the great broch, and Horn had savaged him with words.

"You'd have my people starve?" Horn roared. "They must eat something."

Horn played up to the assembly, and it worked. They muttered their support. They were tired of being hungry and of worrying about being hungry.

Olaf tried to argue, but it was no good.

"If we eat all our wheat now," he said calmly, "then we shall starve."

Horn turned really nasty then.

"If you continue to spread these ill omens, they will come true. The fishing will improve soon, thanks to Gudrun's spells! I suggest you concentrate on finding sea cabbage, the task I gave to you. Then we'd have something to eat!"

Mouse took her blanket with her as she crept out of the grain store at first light. She passed the low stable where Skinfax, Horn's horse, lived. Horn had bartered half a year's worth of wheat for that scraggy horse from some traders. It was the Storn's only horse; they had no use for one, but it was typical of Horn that he should think he needed one. She heard Skinfax give a low whinny as she passed.

"Shhh," she whispered, and put out a calming thought to the animal. He snorted, and Mouse walked on.

She crossed the scrubby fields where they grew the wheat and other stunted vegetables, and made her way up the hills behind the village.

She was heading for the stones on Bird Rock, and within an hour she was there. The sun had climbed with her, and for the first time in weeks it was going to be a warm day. The sun glinted off the sea way below her, casting it a rich blue.

By the time she got to the top of the hill, she was hot. She took her clothes off and flung them in a pile at the foot of one of the huge stones. The stones pointed far away into the sky high above her. They were huge, jagged fingers of rock that formed a rough circle. Some slightly taller or wider than others, there was nothing precise about them.

It was said that however many times you counted them, you would always come up with a different number, but Mouse knew that was rubbish. She counted them often enough to know there were seven of them. They had been there forever—no one knew what they were or who had erected them.

No one else came up here much, only Gudrun, but she never emerged from her tiny hut before midday. It was something to do with being awake late at night making the spells work. The rest of the village feared the place. It seemed a place of magic to them, ancient magic that they did not understand. More than that, it was the place they took their Lawspeakers upon death.

Gudrun, thought Mouse. The Wisewoman. Olaf's hound, Frost, would make a better Wisewoman! The sea gave no fish, the crops were poor, and still everyone put their faith in Gudrun. But in Storn there were reasons for everything, and Gudrun's invulnerable position was no exception to this.

Feeling sorry for herself, Mouse lay in the heather. Instinctively she curled into a ball and began to lick the backs of her hands, as if cleaning them, like a dog, like a wolf, though they were not dirty. After a while she realized what she was doing and made herself stop. Olaf and Freya would be cross if they knew. She rolled onto her back and stared at the sky instead.

There! A crow.

In a moment Mouse left her body and flew up to the bird. With that crow's mind she swung high, surveying the whole coastline. There lay the village. Even from a thousand feet high she could see Olaf setting off with Frost along the shore. What for? She didn't know. There was Freya, pulling a bucket of water from the burn. There was Thorbjorn, the blacksmith, an ally of Olaf's. The village was up and awake now, and there . . . there was the thin figure of Gudrun, leaving Horn's private broch. At this time of the morning! No doubt Horn had been asking her advice on a point of magic.

Magic. What use was Gudrun's magic? Mouse swung away with the crow, which began to head north, along the coast.

This was *real* power.

9

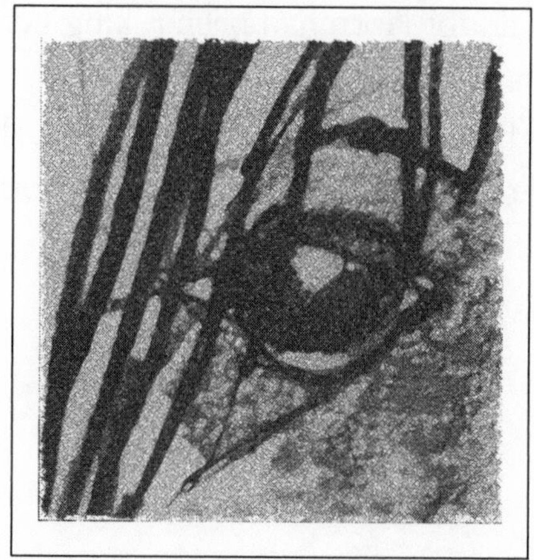

Confusion:

"No, not with words."

"Why haven't you spoken till now?"

"I have, but not with words."

"Then how are we supposed to understand you?"

"The hounds understand me."

"But we're not hounds! How do you speak to them without words?"

"I know what they're thinking. I just need to be near them."

"And is it only dogs?"

"No, not only dogs . . . the wolves . . ."

"You understood them?"

"Why did you hurt them?"

"Did you understand them? How did you come to be with them? What were you before then? How can you speak?"

I watched all this from the back of the crowd. I felt the pain they were subjecting Mouse to, trying to force answers from her. But Mouse had fallen silent.

She would speak no more, would answer no more questions. Whether because she did not want to or because she did not know the answers, I do not know. But the faraway look had come into her face again, and she was silent. As silent as she had been before.

All I sensed in her then was pain, and I wished everyone would leave her alone. As soon as they were busy arguing amongst themselves, I went up to her.

"Mouse?" I said quietly.

She didn't say anything, but she looked at me. Her eyes were filled with tears that did not fall.

"Come with me," I said.

And I took her away from the fuss and the noise, and we walked on the low hills behind the village. The sun was setting.

We sat and watched it sink.

I looked at Mouse and suddenly felt very sorry for her. She was all alone in the land.

She leaned her head on my shoulder.

"Sigurd?" she said.

Somehow I knew what she meant, though she hadn't *spoken* the words.

"Yes," I said, "I will be your brother."

10

"He's gone? He can't have just gone!"

"It's true, Mouse," said Freya. Mouse could see she was trying not to cry anymore. It *was* true.

Olaf stomped around in the background. Frost, the hound, lay exhausted in the corner. They'd walked all day north along the coast but hadn't found Sigurd. No one had seen him since the affair with the box in the great broch.

"I'll go south," said Olaf, "tomorrow."

"No," said Mouse. "Let me look for him. I just need to find a bird to—"

"No," said Olaf sharply.

"But I could search much quicker than—"

"Not that way," said Olaf. "This family is in enough disgrace as it is. If you go parading your . . . *self* in front of everyone, it'll only get worse."

Freya put her hand on Olaf's shoulder.

"But Sigurd . . . ," she began.

"Sigurd's nearly a man now. He can look after himself. And if he can't, well, perhaps it's for the best if he doesn't come back!"

"That's not fair!" cried Mouse, but Olaf stormed out of the broch.

"He doesn't mean it," said Freya, "he doesn't mean it. He loves Sigurd."

Mouse paused.

They were too alike, Olaf and Sigurd, father and son, that was the trouble, said Freya. Both stubborn and proud.

"I know Olaf loves him," Mouse said after a while. "*I* know, but Sigurd doesn't. That's why he's gone, isn't it?"

11

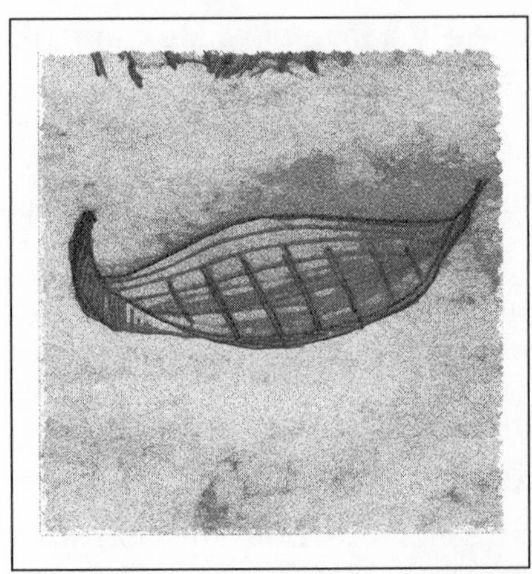

In those first months after she came, we began to learn about Mouse.

I look back now after many years. Horn's plan to saddle my family with a useless, dumb foundling backfired. We didn't fully realize it, but we had in our midst a creature with unheard-of powers. She—Mouse, I mean—was not yet fully in control of her abilities. It appeared that she was learning all the time what she could do.

She sensed things through animals. I have thought about this often, and this is the best way I can explain it. She could use animals, nearby animals, as a channel through which she could feel and see. I still don't know whether she actually saw what the animal saw, or whether she just knew what it was seeing. It doesn't really matter either way. It was an immense power, and unknown, and so? And so, and so, and so, it scared people.

We could have made so much more use of Mouse. Had her

help us. But Horn sensed that people were wary of her, and he fueled their fear.

Once upon a time.

This story will show you what I mean.

Once upon a time the fishermen were returning from the sea, and it had been a bad catch. This was about the time that things started to get difficult for the Storn. When food really started to be hard to come by. When the trading ships were still coming but their stories were full of gloom.

And it was before we started to think about the Dark Horse.

So the fishermen were returning, and it had been a bad catch.

There was a solemn mood amongst those of us milling about on the grass before the great broch. Solemn, but how could we know then how much worse it was going to get?

Mouse was watching. She was next to me.

"Why did they go north?" she said. "The fish are over there."

She pointed to the south of our bay.

"They're only just out to sea," she said.

I looked at her without saying anything, but she had been overheard.

"Hey, Horn," shouted Grinling. "This girl says the fish are that way!"

Horn looked up from where he was talking with one or two men.

"Then let her useless father go and catch them all!" he bawled.

Father had just beached a boat. He heard what Horn said.

For a moment he hesitated, looking at Mouse, looking at Horn, who stared back steadily, aware of everyone watching him.

Something clicked in Father. He was stubborn sometimes. He looked just once more at Mouse, who sat next to me smiling, and then single-handed he dragged the boat back down to the shore.

I hesitated for a while, then ran to help him.

"Go away, Sigurd," he said as I put my hand on the boat.

"You can't do it by yourself," I protested.

He paused. "No need for both of us to make fools of ourselves."

I could tell, though, from the tone of his voice, that he had changed his mind. I climbed aboard, and within seconds we had a sail up that carried us just a couple of hundred yards toward the south of the bay.

Father was quiet.

"Are we really going to try?" I asked.

He held up his hand.

"Cast the nets, Siggy," he said. And a smile grew over his bearded face.

He had sensed the darkness of a huge shoal of fish right under the boat.

When we returned, boat laden with fish, Father and I expected a heroes' welcome, but as we walked up to the broch the eyes of the villagers were filled with dread, not wonder.

"It's not natural," someone muttered.

Father took Mouse by the hand.

"Come, daughter," he said. "It's time we were abed."

I think that was the first time Olaf called Mouse that.

At the time I couldn't understand why people were so scared of Mouse, or rather, of what she could do. After all, wasn't what Gudrun did just the same thing? She was supposed to make magic at the Spell-making—magic to keep us safe, bring us food, and so on and so on. Perhaps it was just that Gudrun's magic was a little less dramatic than Mouse's.

Mouse's magic was harder to believe and easier to fear.

12

Sigurd hadn't meant to run away, but now he had. He'd spent the night shivering in the lee of the goat shed, too humiliated to return to his own broch. Olaf and Freya had not been concerned enough to look for him, believing he would return once he'd calmed down. But as the first light stole into the village, he still hurt too badly to want to see anyone. Knowing people would soon be awake, he left.

He started by heading south down the coast. His father and mother would be snoring in their end of the broch. He didn't know where Mouse was, and he was glad of that. He didn't want to have to face her. He'd let *her* down, too, and he cared most about her.

So he walked in the cool dawn. It was a still, clear morning at the end of Lamb-month; the short summer would soon be upon them. It was going to be a warm day.

He didn't actually mean to run away, but before he'd turned a mile or two under his boots, it came to him that he didn't want to go back. There was nothing for him with the Storn. He didn't want to watch as Horn tormented his father more and more every day.

They'd fought once, years before, when the last Lawspeaker died, and Olaf, Sigurd's father, had lost. That was about six years ago, a summer or two before they found Mouse. And though Horn had won the fight, and though he was Lawspeaker, he was not well liked. He had gathered a group of loyal men around him to secure his position. Olaf said his rule was harsh and stupid; that he was thoughtless and wasteful. There were those who agreed with him, though not openly.

Horn never let Olaf forget that fight, and now that times were difficult, Olaf had become the daily object of his mockery.

Sigurd knew there were other places. Places to the south, large settlements, towns even. He knew this because of the occasional ships that would make their way up the coast in the good weather, bartering with the likes of Horn for whatever good there was to be had. The merchants would sit for a while, telling tales of life in faraway places. Places that sounded so strange it was hard to believe they were real.

Sigurd didn't know if all these stories were true, but he was curious. The villagers of Storn would sit and be still for an hour or so and lap it all up, their eyes widening here and narrowing there as the traders told stories of unimaginable things. Sometimes, very rarely these days, a ship would return past Storn, having ventured into the Northlands. The merchants would say little about these trips but muttered into their beer about fearsome tribesmen with strange ways of living. Strange gods, bizarre religion, and berserkers—battle-crazed warriors who could never be defeated or even hurt.

And horses, there was often mention of horses, and fearsome warriors who rode them.

The Dark Horse.

The merchants would leave, pitching their takings into the hulls of their ships, and the villagers would marvel at their travels and adventures for an hour or so. All except Sigurd, who would yearn a little while longer than the rest.

So Sigurd left his family, and he left his sister, who was not really his sister at all, but who meant something more.

After a while Sigurd recognized where he was. It was about here that he and Mouse had found the box.

He stopped and sat on a rock. For a moment the thought of Mouse hurt him. It was better this way, he decided. She was too timid, too fragile, to go with him, as she would have wanted to. He would miss her, he told himself, half wondering at himself that he was leaving at all.

Was he really leaving?

He would at least have liked to know what was in that box before he left. Now Horn would be showing off whatever treasures it held. And gloating at Olaf more than ever. Sigurd got up off his rock and walked on, and then he heard something behind him.

He turned and screamed.

He fell to the sand.

13

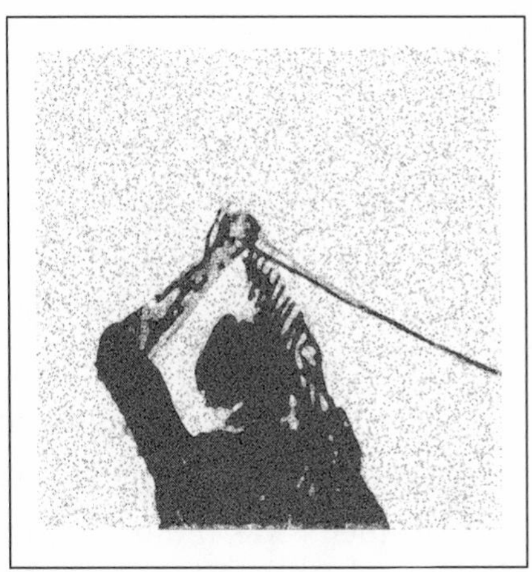

Herda, a gentle, tall man known as the Song-giver, sang. Nearly the whole clan was gathered for the Song-giving, an event that took place whenever the Storn needed entertaining, which was most evenings.

Usually Mouse listened to these songs, captivated. Even after four years with the Storn she still found music a thing to wonder at. But now her mind was on other matters.

She sat quietly, thinking about Sigurd. Though Olaf and Freya were with her, she felt alone without her brother.

"Horn will love this," Olaf whispered grimly to his wife.

Freya knew what he meant. Sigurd's disappearance. Only then did Freya notice something.

Horn.

He was the one other person missing from the great broch. For a moment she wondered why he was not there.

"He ought to have done something," she said to her

husband. "If it were anyone else's boy, he'd have done something."

"I'll go south tomorrow," Olaf said.

He said that yesterday, thought Mouse, overhearing. She knew it was difficult. Anything Olaf did would just be more for Horn to use against them, but surely Siggy was more important. . . .

Never mind what Olaf said. He wasn't really her father anyway. He couldn't stop her. Tomorrow she'd find a bird, an eagle would be best; theirs was the best sight, the longest flight.

She would find Sigurd.

Herda finished his lovely, sad laments and sat down.

Mouse looked down at the fire pit. She feared Olaf was right. Horn was going to use Sigurd's absence to shame Olaf more. Now she noticed his absence, too, but before she had time to wonder at this, he arrived.

He swept through the doorway and down to the fire, where Gudrun and Longshank waited for him.

Then Mouse saw what he was carrying. The box!

She'd forgotten about it; she'd been thinking of only one thing, one person.

What game was Horn playing?

He'd had the box for a day; by now he must have played with, eaten, or otherwise destroyed whatever it contained.

Why bring it here?

Horn placed the box on a stone by the fireside and retreated.

"You!"

He pointed at Mouse. The throng was hushed.

Horn said nothing more, but Mouse knew he wanted her to go to him, by the fire.

There was nothing to do; the Lawspeaker had spoken. So she went. Freya plucked at her woollen skirt as Mouse got up. Mouse caught her eye.

Freya gave her a weak smile, which meant, "Be careful."

Mouse nodded slightly and went. She decided to be careful; she didn't like the feel of this at all. And it also meant going near the fire pit. That in itself made her nervous.

"Lawspeaker?" she said. That was the most formal way of addressing Horn.

"You will open the box."

Mouse was not ready for this. Surely Horn had opened it by now, he must have. Unless . . . supposing he had. He *had* opened it, but there was something bad in it and he wanted *her* to take the blame. The blame for finding it.

"What?" she said without thinking.

Before she knew what had happened, Horn grabbed her by the folds of her cloak and pulled her face toward his.

"Don't try and make a fool of me, girl," he said.

"N-n-no," she stammered, "I just thought you would have."

"I said, don't make a fool of me!" Horn roared. He shoved Mouse away from him so hard that she fell sprawling in the ash by the fire. As she fell her heavy cloak dragged the box from the stone onto the earth floor. She saw Gudrun and Longshank sitting nearby but had no hope for support from them. They were just as much afraid of Horn as she was.

Mouse felt the heat of the fire on her cheeks, but they were burning anyway. From the corner of her eye she saw Olaf stand in anger, but she also saw Freya and Thorbjorn pull him back down.

Horn towered over her.

"Don't make a fool of me. You are trying to play a trick on me! You know I cannot open the box. You will open it."

"No," said Mouse. "No. I didn't know.... Why haven't you opened it? I thought you—"

Horn raised his fist. Mouse quivered.

"I cannot open the box," he growled. Then he glared at Gudrun. "The Wisewoman cannot open the box."

So that was what she had been doing in his broch that morning....

"None of our men can open the box. You found it. You brought it here. Or perhaps it is some game of yours. To make a fool of me!"

No, no, no, thought Mouse.

"So open it!" Horn shouted.

The box lay on the floor between them, in the dust, but it still shone. The firelight made its bloodred wood glow across the space between them. It challenged her.

"Open it!"

Mouse crawled toward the box. She pulled it near and inspected it properly for the first time. No hinges, no catches.

No keyhole, no lock of any sort. Just a faint hint of a join where the lid met the tray of the box itself.

She put her trembling fingers to the top, terrified of what would happen if she failed.

The lid of the box swung smoothly open.

It was empty.

The box was very beautiful inside. It was lined with thin copper sheet, but nevertheless it was utterly empty.

"No!" yelled Horn, raging with frustration, but Mouse knew nothing of this.

She cowered in the dust, shaking, trying not to faint. Something *was* in the box, just not something you could see. Whatever it was tried to take hold of her, and she could feel its power. It was a thing more powerful than even the fire that raged beside her.

"No!" yelled Horn yet again.

Mouse could feel the box start to pull at her mind. Terrified of its force, she tried to get away but couldn't. Her legs wouldn't move, and she felt dizzy; the great hall was spinning around her as if she were drunk. She had to get away but could do nothing.

All in a moment Horn cursed Mouse and drew Cold Lightning, his sword, from its scabbard. He raised the sword above his head. There was a cry from the Storn, some screams. Olaf jumped to his feet and began to push through the gathering.

Horn brought his sword down with all the might of his arms and his back. On the box.

And his sword broke in two. The broken part spun away

off the ground and flew across the fire pit. There was a cry. It had cut Gudrun. Horn stood quivering with rage, clutching the stump of his weapon loosely in one hand. Dumbly he loosed his grip and the broken blade slid to the earth. Horn was staring at the box.

He picked it up. He had hit it square and true. Cold Lightning lay broken on the floor, but there was not the slightest mark on the wooden box.

In frustration he slammed its lid shut and stormed from the great broch.

As he did so Mouse felt the presence of the box vanishing, and she was left, shaking with fear, in the dirt by the fire.

14

Gudrun did not seem to be too badly hurt. The broken edge of Cold Lightning had sliced through her dress and made a messy cut across her stomach, but it was not deep. But she was the Wisewoman. She was the one who mended arms and delivered babies. The one who tended people's wounds. There was no one to look after her.

15

The white man picked up Sigurd's body and carried him across his shoulders like a dead deer. He felt cold again, though it was a warm day. His head swam a little every now and again, and he had to stop. Sweat ran freely from his face.

The boy couldn't have come far from where he lived. He had nothing with him—no pack, no food, nothing. He hoisted the boy's body higher onto his shoulders and set off along the coast, north. Back the way the boy had come.

16

There were times when we'd have been truly lost without Mouse.

I was away when Horn's sword tip flew across the fire pit and cut Gudrun. Mouse told me all about it later. She seemed confused and told the story badly. She was upset because I had run away.

I was stupid. It still shames me to think that I ran away from the village. I don't suppose I really meant to go anywhere, but I went far enough to cause trouble, and while I was gone, Gudrun got hurt by Horn's anger and impatience.

17

The morning after the sword broke, Horn summoned Mouse. Forlornly she walked around the side of the great broch to the Lawspeaker's dwelling. Standing not too far away from the great meeting place was the next most impressive broch in the village. This broch was larger than the ones the other Storn lived in and was also different in that it was not round, but a long rectangle. This gave it the sense of having two distinct ends inside, almost like two rooms.

Mouse was miserable. She had tried to find Sigurd and had failed.

She'd had no trouble finding a bird, not an eagle as she'd hoped, but a sparrow hawk. Nearly every bit as good. She'd spotted it away to the south, heading down the coast, just as she'd needed. But as she had lain on her back on the high hill she'd flown as far as she could before she lost contact with the bird, and she had neither seen nor felt a single hint of Sigurd.

Either he was dead or injured and she could not reach him, or he had traveled far and fast. Neither of these things made Mouse happy, and as a result she cared little about why Horn had called her to him.

Horn stared at Mouse for a long time. While she waited, Mouse looked around her, rather than meet his searching eyes. Horn's broch was not only larger than the others, it was also very different inside. It seemed to contain more possessions than the rest of Storn put together. The walls were hung with all manner of things—weapons, clothes, pots... too many things to take in at one go. Mouse guessed that these were the belongings of all the previous Lawspeakers who had lived here. The floor was more richly covered than any she had seen before, with thick, many-colored rugs.

When he finally did speak, Horn mentioned neither the box nor Sigurd.

Picking his words carefully, now Horn did not look her in the eye.

"Gudrun has asked for you. You will do as she says. Follow her instructions carefully."

Mouse scratched her nose. This was something. It was obviously very irritating to Horn to have to ask for Mouse's help again. The second time in just a few hours, and the last time had ended badly for Horn. Mouse had heard people complaining about him openly; the atmosphere in the village was becoming more and more strained.

Horn seemed to have finished speaking. Mouse dared to ask a question.

"What am I to do?"

"Gudrun is hurt. She has asked that you nurse her wound. You will do what she says. There is nothing more to say. Go to her now."

Mouse went.

18

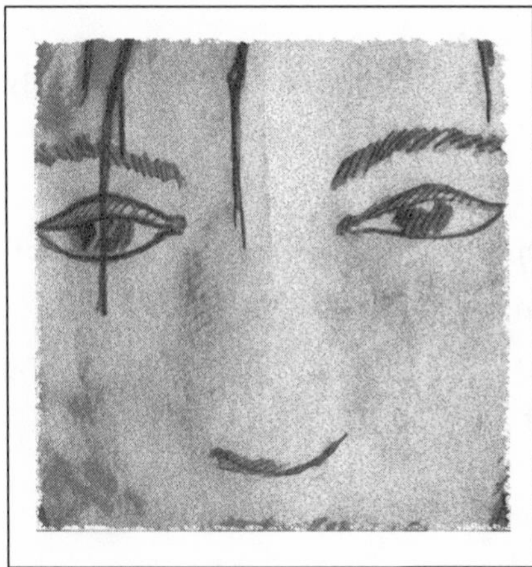

I had promised to be Mouse's brother. I knew it meant more than that. She wanted someone who would be true to her, always. Dependable. Someone whom she could trust. I had let her down.

Why was this so important to her? I had begun to find out a little. About her time with the wolves. Though nothing about the time before that. But it was difficult because she never seemed to want to talk about things much.

One day, though, as we were gathering sea cabbage in the high-tide line she said, "Sig, how long have you lived here?"

I didn't understand the question at first. At least, I thought I must have missed something.

"All my life, of course. Why?"

She shrugged and said nothing, but a few minutes later she spoke again, without looking up.

"So Freya and Olaf have always been your mother and father, then?"

"Of course."

She said nothing more, but I thought it might be worth trying to ask her a question or two.

"Who were your parents, Mouse?"

The answer she gave me brought a chill to my heart and a lump to my throat.

"The wolves," she said, and threw another piece of seaweed into our basket.

19

"Where's your brother, then?"

It was Sif. She'd been hanging around outside her father's broch. Waiting to ambush Mouse. Mouse had managed to avoid her since she produced the box at the Spell-making. But there was no avoiding her now.

"Well?" she said spitefully. "Where is he? I thought you two went everywhere together."

Mouse ignored her and tried to walk past, but Sif blocked her way.

"Don't ignore me."

Why now, why? thought Mouse. Leave me alone.

Sif was nearly as old as Sigurd and was much taller than Mouse. Mouse knew from experience that she was stronger, too.

"Things to do, Sif. Let me past."

"Who do you think I am? Don't try to ignore me. You

and your stupid brother, you think you're stronger than me? You're wrong!"

Mouse's lips quivered. She hated herself. She was so weak, she couldn't even take being bullied by this fool.

"I'm busy, Sif. Your father—"

"How did you open the box?" demanded Sif, angrier now.

"Be quiet," said Mouse without thinking.

Sif hit Mouse across the face with the back of her hand. Mouse dropped to the ground, holding her cheek. She felt blood rush into her face, and she looked up to see Sif glaring at her. Anger and joy made her ugly. She spat at Mouse.

"Get up," she said. "No one tells me to be quiet."

Mouse looked up at Sif, who was ready to strike again.

"Why do you hate me?" she asked.

This stopped Sif for a moment. Mouse looked at her. She was the Lawspeaker's daughter. She was actually quite beautiful, with long, straight, dark hair. She was also cleverer than many of the villagers. She had a lot she could be happy about, and Mouse did not understand why she wasted so much time picking on her.

Sif stamped her foot.

"Get up!" she shouted.

Mouse stayed where she was.

"You and that boy!" Sif said.

She meant Sigurd. Her statement was without apparent meaning, but in reality full of a message to be heard. Now Sif made as if to kick Mouse where she sat. But Sif hadn't seen her father standing behind her, and as she took the step toward Mouse he swept Sif off her feet with his boot.

Sif made an unintelligible noise and rolled over. She cried a little girl's cry.

"Father!"

"Go inside, Sif," said Horn.

"But she should tell us how she—"

"Inside. Now."

There was a brief moment in which Sif decided to keep her mouth shut. She flung an angry look at Mouse but did as Horn said.

He turned to Mouse.

"Thank you . . . ," Mouse began.

"I thought I gave you a job to do," said Horn.

Mouse ran to Gudrun's hut.

20

Things got easier for Mouse once we gave her work to do. After she'd been found sleeping with the dogs, Father decided that it would be better if she helped do something. That way someone could always keep an eye out for her.

She seemed happier once she had things to do, though Horn saw to it that she did only the most menial work. I wanted to be with her, so I gave up my place in the prow of one of the fishing boats. It meant I was giving up the prestige that could one day have been mine—in charge of a boat—but I was happy to do it, even if it did mean hunting for scraps in the tide line. I remember those early days with some fondness. I would watch Mouse moving easily and stealthily across the rock pools and marvel at her. For a while you could forget she had grown up living as a wolf, and then something like that would remind me that I really knew so little about her.

And Mouse began to talk more, and we grew up together, though she stayed small and delicate, while I grew as tall as I am now. And she never lost the strange edge to her voice. Another reminder of her past, of those years when she couldn't have uttered a single sound. Well, not a human one, anyway.

Still, she wouldn't say much about her early life. I think she didn't know that much. On several occasions I found her crying. The first time I was really frightened by it.

"What's wrong?" I asked, but she wouldn't reply.

"What's wrong, Mouse?" I asked again and again, until finally she replied.

"Bad dreams," she said.

She told me a little, but only a little.

"Darkness," she said. "Darkness all the time. I'm alone on a hill in the darkness."

"But you like the darkness," I said, thinking about when she had first arrived, how she had always tried to find dark places to sleep, to be.

She nodded.

"Yes," she said, "I do. That's not what's wrong. . . ."

But she couldn't, or wouldn't, tell me what was.

Bad dreams, she'd said, but I wonder now if they weren't actually bad *memories*.

Things were good for a few years after Mouse came. She grew up with us, and one Lamb-month would pass into the summer, and then Harvest-month would pass into the slaughtering of the sheep in Blood-month, and we'd find ourselves in the long winter.

I can remember evenings in our broch, when things were well. Olaf sitting, resting after a hard day's work. Freya cooking and seeing to the fire. Mouse and I playing on the floor. I showed her many things, things that were simple enough to me but that seemed to be magic to Mouse.

I showed her the way to tie the knots that made our fishing nets. She stared in wonder as I made a tiny net from some woollen thread of Freya's. She laughed, and Freya and Olaf laughed with her. I stared at the strange girl who had become my sister as she held the toy net up to her face by the firelight and tried to see how it had been done.

"Time to eat now," Freya would say when our games were done, and eat we did, for there was no hunger then.

And the pattern of the years repeated itself again, and things were well enough. But then the world began to change, and the suffering began.

At first it was just harsher weather. Cold, wet winters followed by barren, rainless summers. Crops failed too often, and no one could explain why. The sheep went hungry and many lambs never survived even halfway to Blood-month. And the fish—that was the worst part. Day after day could pass without a single decent catch.

It put the Storn under pressure. It was like a tinderbox waiting for a spark, and I think now that the spark was when we found the box. Take one example. Horn, who had never been the most coolheaded of men, was driven crazy by the thing. It tormented him. And the result? The tip of his sword lands in Gudrun's stomach. He injures the Wisewoman, so important to so many of us.

But it was to be worse yet for Horn.

21

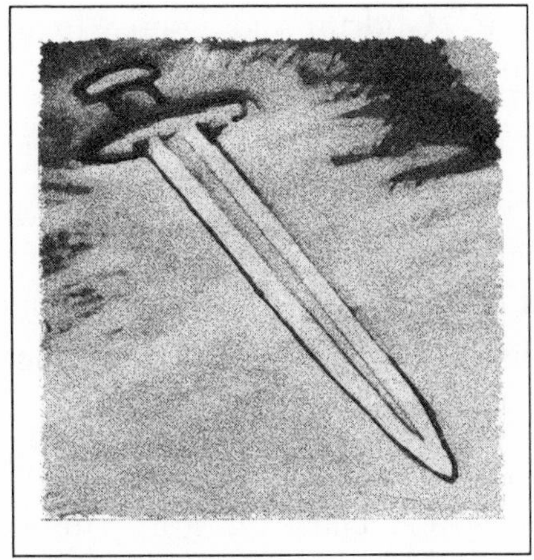

It smelt in Gudrun's hut. Partly it was the smell of her wound, which was turning bad, but there was a mixture of other smells, too. Mouse had caught whiffs of them before, but never had she tasted them so strongly. Herbs. Herbs hanging from the ceiling to dry, with other less pleasant things. Bits of animals.

All for Spell-making, thought Mouse. Gudrun's type of spells, anyway.

"Come here."

Mouse heard a quiet voice in the darkness. There was Gudrun, lying on a low bed of heather by the far wall. She looked thinner than ever.

Mouse wasn't exactly scared of Gudrun. She didn't fear her because she was a Wisewoman, like some of the Storn did, and she didn't fear her because she was frightening. But Horn treated Gudrun as an ally, and that was enough to put Mouse on her guard.

"Come here," Gudrun said again. "I can't speak any louder. Here. By the bed."

Mouse knelt by Gudrun's bed. "What do you want me to do?"

"Listen. I know you don't trust me. . . ."

Mouse sat up straight. Perhaps she had underestimated Gudrun's abilities. It was as if she'd just read her mind.

"No. I—"

"No, you don't," said Gudrun, trying to lift her head to look at Mouse. "Well. That's all right. I'm not sure I trust you, either. So we're even."

Gudrun paused, out of breath. She winced and put her head back on her pillow.

"That's right?" she pressed.

"Yes," said Mouse. She could not see any harm in admitting it.

"You don't trust me because I have Horn's confidence," Gudrun stated. She knew it was true, and Mouse didn't bother denying it.

"Well," Gudrun continued, "let me tell you. If you're the Wisewoman to a tribe, it's pretty important that the Lawspeaker trust you."

Mouse nodded, but she wasn't sure what Gudrun was getting at. She waited.

"I know you have powers," said Gudrun. She watched Mouse to see if her words had any effect.

"I . . . I can do things," said Mouse, struggling a little for words. "Some things other people can't."

"Yes," said Gudrun. "Exactly."

She paused again, to wait for the pain to pass. "That's why you're here. You're the one person in this whole . . . this tribe that might be able to save me."

Mouse said nothing.

"When was the last time anyone died during childbirth?" Gudrun went on. "When was the last time anyone died because of a wound going bad? You can't remember because it hasn't happened in a long, long time. I'm very good at what I do, with my herbs and powders. So listen. It's a long time, but unless you do what I tell you, I'll be the next. See?"

Mouse nodded. She stared at the mess that was Gudrun's stomach.

22

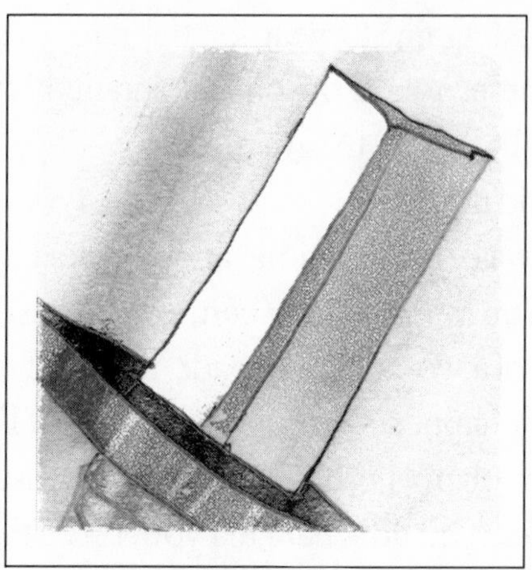

So, like I say, Mouse grew up into the life of the village, though maybe there were some who never fully accepted her. Horn and Sif, obviously, but I think there were others, too.

Even when she made Gudrun well again, there were still some who feared Mouse. I suppose they had good reason to fear her, in a way.

That time with the fish, when Mouse told us where the fish were, and she was right.

There were other things, too, like her sleeping with the hounds, and I remember a time once when I surprised her accidentally. I was sleeping in our broch one afternoon when she came in. I woke slowly and got up. She hadn't heard me, I suppose, because as I sat down next to her she leaped to her feet, snarling. Like, I can only say, like a wolf; lips drawn back, teeth showing. In an instant the look slipped from her face and she was a normal girl again.

That kind of thing happened on other occasions, and it was

disturbing if you thought about it that way. But we could have used her, used her skills, to help us through the tough times.

Tough times! At least then it was only that food was hard to come by. The Dark Horse were no more than an old legend to us then. But it wouldn't be long.

23

Mouse had done everything Gudrun had asked of her, and it had taken a long time.

Gudrun's fire had gone out. That was the first thing. Mouse fetched a brand from the fire pit in the great broch to get it going again. Back in the hut she put her worries about Sigurd in the back of her mind and started the healing magic.

Under Gudrun's instruction from the bed, Mouse took a branch of one of Gudrun's herbs—sea rose, she called it. She chopped its tiny fingers of leaves and shoots until there was no piece larger than an ant. She did the same with a plant Gudrun called groundsel. Then she set the leaves to boil in a small pot in the fire. While that was stewing, she cleaned Gudrun's wound. It had gone very bad very quickly.

"Dirty blade," said Gudrun, trying to ignore the pain as Mouse pulled the sodden cloth from the wound.

"Dirty?" asked Mouse.

"That slob! Horn," said Gudrun. "It's dirty blades that make wounds fester this quick."

Mouse stared at her.

"No, not evil magic. Dirt. That slob can't even keep the Lawspeaker's sword clean. Now look what he's done to me!"

Mouse trotted down to the sea to fetch a bowl of water. With this she cleaned the wound. Not deep, but messy. That was the trouble.

"Lots of nasty corners for the dirt to hide in," said Gudrun.

Then, again doing just what Gudrun told her, Mouse made a small amount of bread dough with the herb stew from the pot and a little oat flour. Gudrun was able to help press this dough straight onto her wound. A clean cloth to cover it.

"We're done," said Gudrun.

"Don't we... you have to say some magic?" asked Mouse.

"No. That's it. Same again tomorrow."

Mouse started to leave.

"Mouse," Gudrun said, stopping her.

"What is it?"

"Tell me something," Gudrun said. Sif was not the only one who had thought about what had happened just before Gudrun's accident.

"How did you open the box?" she asked.

Mouse said nothing.

"Horn tried to open it. He got *me* to try to open it. *No one* could open it until you just lifted the lid. How?"

But Mouse shook her head. "I must go. You must rest."

"How?" asked Gudrun again.

"I don't know," Mouse said, and left.

24

Mouse. Olaf and Herda. Sif. All of them and many others ran from their brochs the moment they heard the cry. More soon joined them, including Freya.

"Stranger coming!"

It was true. A tall, thin, white-haired man had just walked openly into the center of the cluster of brochs. There was something slung over his shoulders. Then he stumbled and fell. He slumped to the ground, and his burden tumbled to the turf and rolled a foot or so.

"Sigurd!" cried Mouse.

She ran to him. Freya knelt down beside him, too.

Olaf took a step forward, then hesitated. He looked to the sky.

"Sigurd?" mouthed Freya.

Mouse felt his chest with her tiny hand. "He's breathing!"

"Thank you," said Olaf under his breath. He strode over to where his son lay and scooped him off the springy turf.

"Where's Horn?" he barked at the people standing around.

No one answered.

"Well, until he shows up, lock that man in the grain barn."

He nodded at the white-haired man, who hadn't moved since he'd fallen, then he carried Sigurd inside. Only Mouse saw the tear roll down Olaf's rough cheek. She smiled.

There was a moment when no one did anything. Then Freya stood.

"You heard what Olaf said," she murmured, and followed her husband. Mouse watched as a couple of men carried the stranger into the grain barn. Then she hurried after Freya.

25

Ragnald. The man with the white hair and the black palms. He was a mystery from the start, and he stayed that way.

His hair had gone white from the frost, he said, and the frost had blackened his palms. He'd been traveling for years, through the cold lands of the north, slowly coming south. And he knew about the box. He said that it was his and that it contained magic of all sorts. (Except we knew it was empty.)

I don't know which of this was true, nor does it matter much now.

26

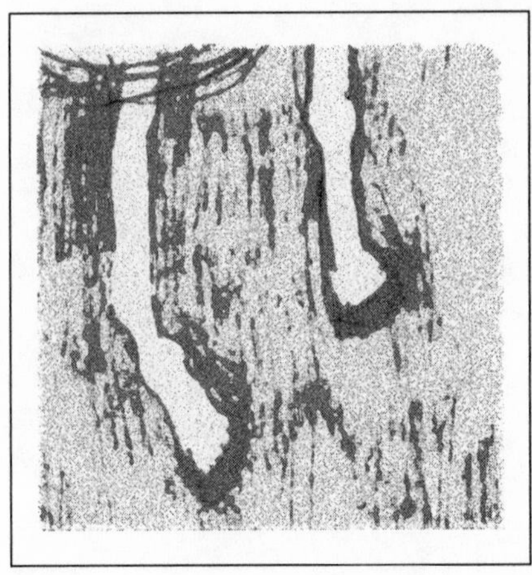

Sigurd was unconscious. The man with white hair was not.

"Hey!" he called from the grain barn. "Let me out!"

Someone was sent to find Horn.

"I won't hurt you! Won't you even talk to me?"

After a while Horn came out to see what was going on. He staggered a little, as if he'd been drinking.

"Well, where is he?"

"In the barn, Horn," one of his men said.

"Well, get him out. Let's see him. Have your weapons ready, mind."

Mouse, who had come to the door of the broch to watch, didn't know whether to laugh or cry as she saw Horn's finest warriors gird their loins, and their swords, in the face of a single stranger.

The man stepped out cautiously. He looked around him, and he looked different. The villagers, almost all light brown or blond haired, had never seen pure white hair before. And he was nearly a foot taller than their tallest man.

He looked from one face to another, then approached Horn, apparently having worked out that he was the leader.

"Mighty Chief, I mean no harm, I simply—"

"No farther, stranger!"

Horn drew his own sword but remembered too late that he had broken Cold Lightning on the box. He waved the stump at the man, pretending it was what he had meant to do. Mouse saw Herda shaking his head grimly. At least there was the strong Thorbjorn, with his smith's hammer, standing nearby.

"My noble lord," the man tried again, "I am a simple traveler; I mean no harm."

"What is your name, stranger? Where are you from?"

"From the south. A city far to the south. Skerry. No doubt a lord as great as yourself will have heard of it?"

Horn swayed on his feet a little.

"Of course," he said after a moment.

"Great Lord, my name is Ragnald. I am a simple traveler and was caught in a shipwreck not far down the shore from here."

He paused. Mouse watched as Horn and Ragnald sized each other up. Surely the stranger could tell Horn was drunk?

"My noble lord, I mean no harm. I found the boy—"

"The boy!" Horn said suddenly, finding something he could threaten the man with. "What did you do to the boy? You would harm one of my people?"

He took an unsteady, though menacing, step toward Ragnald. He was still waving his sword stump.

"No," said Ragnald, "I found him. Indeed, I saved him. Why would I bring him back here if I meant him ill? Your Lordship is wise to mistrust a stranger," he added quickly.

Horn thought about this.

"What," he said eventually, "are you doing here?"

For the first time the newcomer was short of words.

"I . . . am a . . . an entertainer," he said after a pause. "Yes! I have entertained many people in many lands, across all the seas and islands. The poor and the weak, the rich and the strong. Great rulers, like yourself. I have traveled far, and often I have exchanged a story or two for a bed. And now I find myself here. . . ."

He smiled at Horn, but showing utmost respect.

"I see," said Horn uncertainly.

"I don't see," said a voice from behind Mouse. Olaf pushed past her and strode out into the center of things. Murmurs spread through the crowd.

Olaf walked right up to Ragnald, until his face was just a foot away from the white-haired man's.

"My boy is lying hurt in there," said Olaf. "He will not wake. Just what happened? Tell me that!"

But Horn regained his grip.

"Olaf! Get away! I am in charge here! Or would you like to take our friend's place in the grain?"

Some of Horn's men closed around Olaf a little. He laughed at them, but he did as he was told.

Horn turned back to the stranger. "You. Rag . . . ?"

"Ragnald, my lord."

"Ragnald. What kind of entertainer are you?"

"I am sorry to say that at present I am a very poor entertainer, for everything I need is contained in a box. A very special wooden box. I lost it when I was cast ashore. Have you, by any chance, seen such a thing?"

The man gestured with his hands as he spoke. Now the shape they held, invisibly, was the box. Then he shrugged, his black palms up. As the people saw them they drew breath, wondering what disease or experience had caused this bizarre disfigurement.

There was a long silence. People stared at Horn. Horn stared at his people.

"No," he said. "No, we have found nothing like that."

The man studied Horn's face for a moment longer than perhaps he should have, but after a moment more he spoke.

"Then I am a very poor entertainer indeed, for the box contains magics of all kinds, and without it I am nothing."

27

I can remember that I woke screaming.

In my head I was back at the beach.

I remember Mother came over and held me; Father crouched at the foot of my bed, staring at me. I can see myself now as the boy I was then, shivering with fear. How quickly I was to grow up!

"Shhh," said my mother. "Shhh, my boy."

After a while I stopped screaming. The beach seemed a little farther away, the beach with the black horses bearing down on me. . . .

"What is it, Sig?" asked Mouse.

She sat by me, waiting quietly.

And so I told them all about the horses. I was ashamed because I'd been running away, and they knew that. It remained unspoken.

One moment I had been walking along the beach.

Strangely, I had heard nothing until I turned and saw the stampede of black horses about to trample me into the sand.

"Horses!" exclaimed Freya.

"Where did they come from?" asked Olaf.

I shook my head.

"And that man was riding them?" asked Father.

"Which man?" I replied. I didn't know who he was talking about. "There was no one. Just the horses—no, wait. I did see a face, just once. I remember being lifted up."

"Then the stranger is a good man," said my mother. "He brought you back to us! Olaf, you must thank him."

Father nodded. I learned later how he had challenged Ragnald, but that was a good thing about my father. He was honest and could admit to his mistakes.

"Yes," he agreed. "I have a lot to thank him for."

Then Father put out his huge hand and held mine with it.

I felt foolish and small, but deeply loved.

I looked at Mouse, who had a peculiar look on her face. Only for a moment, and then it was gone.

"Horses?" she said quietly.

28

"Tell me what is going on, Mouse," said Gudrun.

Mouse had tended to the Wisewoman's wounds many times now. An uneasy friendship had developed between them. Gudrun was grateful for the careful way Mouse followed her instructions. This time Mouse had remembered how to make the poultice perfectly, without any help from the Wisewoman. She placed it gently on Gudrun's wound.

"You see?" said Gudrun.

"Yes. It's much better already."

"No, Mouse. I mean do you see what you can do? I'd only have to teach you."

Mouse said nothing, just smiled. She still didn't trust Gudrun, didn't understand her motives. In a way they were quite alike. Both of them stood a little outside the village in general. Mouse because she was a foundling, Gudrun because of her calling. The villagers respected Gudrun because of her importance to them; they were also afraid of her. Their attitude toward Mouse was not so different. Mouse felt this instinctively but also knew that the person Gudrun had most contact with was someone to be feared. Horn.

"Wouldn't you like to know the things I can do?" asked Gudrun.

Mouse shrugged, and smiled again.

"If only I could do what you can do," said Gudrun.

Mouse stopped smiling. She didn't want to think about that at the moment. It hadn't kept Sigurd out of trouble or helped find him.

"So what's going on?"

"That man. Ragnald. He says he found Sigurd lying on the beach."

"What does Sigurd say?" asked Gudrun.

"He doesn't remember much, and he's still sleeping a lot. I don't know what happened to him. He says he was run down by horses. Black horses."

"Black horses?" repeated Gudrun slowly. She, too, had heard the legend. "There aren't many horses around here. We're lucky enough to have Skinfax."

"But Gudrun, that's not all. He has white hair and black palms. And the box! You know, that—"

"Yes," said Gudrun. The thought of the box reminded her of her accident. She winced. "What of it?"

"The box is his!"

Gudrun seemed unmoved by this. "Has Horn given it back to him?"

"No," said Mouse. "That's a strange thing. Horn pretended we didn't have it."

Gudrun laughed.

"And the stranger said it contains his magic tricks," Mouse continued. "He says he is an entertainer, but we know the box is empty, and yet Horn has let this pass. He seems to like the stranger."

Gudrun was silent for a while. She managed to pull herself up in her bed without too much pain.

"Has Horn done anything about Cold Lightning yet?"

"Thorbjorn says it can't be mended. He must forge a new sword."

"That will hurt him," said Gudrun, meaning Horn. "That sword has been passed from one Lawspeaker to the next for generations. No new sword will be the same."

Mouse nodded. True, she thought. Things were not the same. There was a subtle shift taking place. People were talking about Horn behind his back quite openly. The nucleus of his henchmen was closing around him, and he had even taken the stranger, Ragnald, into his broch on more than one occasion. It was undeniable that many of the Storn were beginning to show their mistrust of Horn.

"Mouse," said Gudrun, "there's one more thing—you'll have to help give the Spell-making tonight."

"No. I can't," said Mouse automatically. The thought of sitting in front of the whole tribe made her feel sick. The thought of sitting near the fire pit still made her feel uneasy. "I couldn't."

"Yes, you can. I can't speak loud enough. I'll get them to

carry me to the great broch. I'll whisper to you, and you can recite the lines to everyone."

Mouse shivered and looked at Gudrun.

"You'll do it," said Gudrun. "You must do as I say. Horn has told you that, hasn't he?"

29

"Sig. I have to give the Spell-making tonight."

Mouse.

I'd been sitting, feeling sorry for myself. Feeling stupid for running away. I had got nowhere, and I felt I was still going nowhere. I had spent the day digging up shriveled potatoes. And I remember thinking then that things were bad not just for me. The fishing was worse than ever; the crops were failing.

I was sitting on one of the grassy banks behind the great broch, watching the sea. Mouse came over.

"I have to give the Spell-making," she said.

I nodded.

"I know," I said.

"Who told you?"

"Ragnald."

"Ragnald!" she said. "How did he know?"

I shook my head.

"Horn seems to like him," I ventured.

"He scares me, Sig," she said. "There's something about him that scares me."

"He saved my life, Mouse," I said. "Doesn't that count for something?"

I said this, but I felt something of her fear, too. He was strange. But I seemed to have won the point with Mouse.

"Yes, of course it does," she said. "Don't be angry with me. I'm just worried."

"About the Spell-making?" I asked.

"Hmm," she said. "The Spell-making."

So that was it.

"Don't worry, you'll be fine. In fact, you'll be wonderful. You're going to be something special, Mouse. With your skill, your mind."

"No," said Mouse, and she shook her head. "I don't want to."

"Yes," I said. "You will. While I go on finding seaweed and growing potatoes."

She put her hand on my arm.

"Sigurd," she said, but I was not in the mood to listen.

"I'm going inside," I said.

I left.

As I ducked under the low doorway of the broch I saw that Sif had been watching all this. She scowled at me.

For once I failed to ignore her.

"What?" I said aggressively.

"Troubles?" she said slyly.

"None of your concern."

"Perhaps I can help?"

She seemed to be playing a game. I shouldn't have said what I said next, but I was too angry to care.

"The only thing you can do is tell your father to sort this village out before we starve."

"How dare you!" she said.

"It's nothing but the truth!" I answered. "Tell me it isn't true. Tell me we're not in trouble."

She was silent. Amazingly, she looked worried.

"Is it really bad?" she asked, as if she'd never thought about it before.

Expecting another of her tricks, I paused for a moment. But I could see no game this time.

"I don't know," I told her honestly, "but if it goes on like this, we'll starve before summer's here. Your father gave a whole bucketful of grain to Skinfax the other day. I saw him."

Again she seemed dumbfounded, almost shocked. So unlike the Sif I was used to.

"We're eating too much of the grain," she agreed. "But Skinfax must eat."

"He'll end up eating that horse," I said bitterly.

I left.

30

Again Mouse found herself in the center of the great broch. She was not in trouble, but she was more scared than when Horn had raised his sword above her head. For this time she had to speak in front of the whole tribe of the Storn.

She looked around. With most of the light in the broch coming from the fire beside her, she noticed that it was actually quite difficult to see all the faces staring at her. Those at the front were clear enough, however.

There was Horn, glaring. Mouse looked away. She knew she had Gudrun to thank for this—Horn was simply tolerating his Wisewoman's decision. Mouse was not surprised when she saw Ragnald, the white stranger, sitting near Horn. Ragnald had been keeping Horn amused with tales of his travels as an entertainer, and Horn had elevated the stranger to a position of privilege.

Mouse had not seen Ragnald do any entertaining herself.

She saw Freya, who mouthed something at her, she

couldn't tell what, though she knew what she meant. She was wishing her well. Next to Freya sat Olaf. She couldn't see Sigurd. He had to be here, though, because the whole tribe had to be.

They waited. There was a commotion at the doorway, and then the deer-hide curtain was pulled back to allow someone to pass. Sif came first, her hands by her sides. Then Mouse realized she was carrying the front end of a stretcher-like bed. On the bed lay Gudrun. And then Mouse saw that the back end was being carried by Sigurd.

She had no time to wonder at this strange union, for the bed was placed beside her, between her and Horn.

Horn shifted uncomfortably, and suddenly it occurred to Mouse that Gudrun was playing games with him.

"You. Lawspeaker," said Gudrun. "You are responsible for this. You wounded me—now I humiliate you. Here is your daughter and the son of your enemy united in carrying me. And here is Mouse, the one you fear, the one you hate, performing the sacred spells. So I humiliate you!"

Mouse looked at Gudrun. And with a shock she realized Gudrun had not said a word. She was lying on the bed, struggling to sit upright with the help of Sigurd and Sif.

But Mouse had heard Gudrun's thoughts clearly, and it put a smile onto her face. She felt a little courage creep into her.

"Mouse," said Gudrun quietly. This time for real, in her real, broken, wound-weakened voice.

Mouse nodded.

"Let's begin," said Gudrun.

31

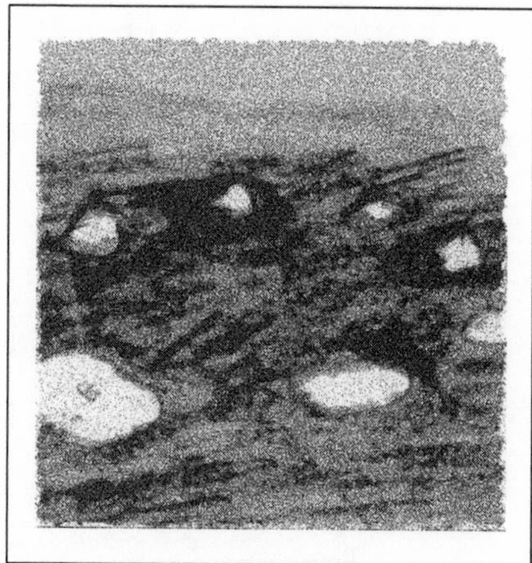

When Gudrun asked me to carry her into the broch for the Spell-making, I jumped at the chance to do something important. Something different.

Of course, she didn't tell me who she'd asked to carry the other end until it was too late to back down without shame.

And from the look on Sif's face I guess Gudrun had pulled the same trick on her.

I didn't know what she was up to—Gudrun, I mean. Not then. Playing her own games, maybe. But thinking about it now, I see what she was doing.

32

Mouse gave the Spell-making, and all was well. She took her usual place at the edge of the circles of people.

Then Horn signaled for Herda to give a song, which he did. At the end of the song Mouse turned to see if Ragnald had been impressed, but he had gone. He must have left during the singing. Horn sat glowering in the firelight. Herda hesitated, unsure of what to do, until Horn grabbed a handful of dirt from the floor and threw it angrily into the fire.

The broch emptied rapidly.

33

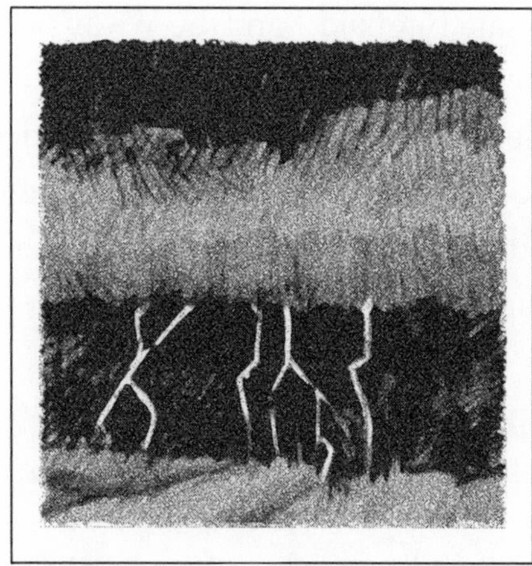

And how strange things became, so quickly then.

Sif and Sigurd carried Gudrun on her stretcher once more, this time back to her bed. Before they were halfway back, Gudrun was asleep, exhausted with the effort of the Spell-making.

There was an uneasy silence between them. Both pretended to be quiet for Gudrun's sake, to avoid having to engage in the usual hostilities.

As they left Gudrun's hut a figure stepped in front of them.

"Good evening," said Ragnald.

Sigurd said nothing. Sif looked sideways at him and was silent, too.

"That was brave work," he went on.

Hardly. But Sif swallowed the bait.

"My father is Lawspeaker," she said pointlessly.

"Indeed," said Ragnald, "and the Wisewoman chose you well. Both of you."

Sig was silent still. Sif gave him another sideways glance. It passed through Sigurd's mind that he no longer felt grateful to Ragnald for saving his life. He wondered when the change had happened and why. He had begun to distrust the stranger.

Ragnald spoke again.

"It seems to me that you two are the finest of the tribe here. . . ."

"My father—" began Sif, but Ragnald held up a hand.

"Indeed," he said. "What I mean to say is that you are the finest of the young people of the Storn. You are ambitious! You have strong wills!"

He waited a moment for his words to ring in their ears.

"I suppose," he continued, "it won't be long before you are the Lawspeaker here, Sif?"

"The Lawspeaker is always a man," she said bitterly.

"Always?" asked Ragnald. "Then who will take charge when your father . . . ?"

"There will be a fight."

Ragnald nodded. "As there was between your fathers. Correct?"

Sigurd grew uneasy. He didn't like this line of questioning.

"You've learned a lot about us already," he said.

Ragnald shrugged. "Perhaps you would walk with me and tell me more?"

He glanced down to the beach, where the moon lit a silver path out to sea.

Sig stood where he was, motionless.

Sif spoke.

"Of course," she said. "As I am the Lawspeaker's daughter, it is my duty to make guests welcome."

And Sigurd thought again that maybe he was being unfair to Ragnald. Hadn't he saved his life? Then he spoke quickly, before Sif's words were cold.

"As one who owes you his life, I am honored to walk with you, Ragnald."

"Ah," he said. "You speak like kings! Let's walk. . . ."

So the three strolled down to the moonlit beach, the stones and sand crunching underfoot.

34

Mouse was looking for Sigurd. Freya had gone to bed, Olaf to the drinking in the great broch, but their son was nowhere to be found.

She looked in at the door of Gudrun's hut, but the Wisewoman was sleeping soundly; Sigurd and Sif were long gone.

The desire to see Sigurd began to overwhelm her. She had been unsettled by Ragnald. She *needed* to see her brother.

Though she was forbidden to do it, she walked quickly but quietly over to the small stone house where the female hounds were sent when they were having pups. She knew there was a mother in there now.

"Shhh, Moss," she said at the low doorway.

The dog stirred and lifted its head as Mouse crawled inside. The feeling of protection and calm in the kennel cheered Mouse immediately.

“Are these your pups?” Mouse asked the dog. She tickled one under the ear.

“I need your help, Moss,” Mouse said. “Lie still.”

Mouse lay down next to the dog, which continued to suckle its newborn, undisturbed.

“What can you hear, Moss?” whispered Mouse. “What can you hear?”

35

Imagine you're standing at the top of a hill. It's a very steep hill, and beside you is a large rock. A boulder, huge and round and heavy. Now, put the sole of your foot against the rock as it stands on the brink of the hill. Push, push hard, and the boulder starts to roll down the hill. It moves slowly at first, as if unsure of what it will do, but then it speeds up, until it hurtles headlong into the future. Nothing can stop it now.

Well, this is what happened to us. Everything that was about to happen was unstoppable and would change our lives forever.

I walked beside Sif. I was wary of her, but I did not want to be outdone by her. A step behind and between us walked Ragnald.

"So, my lord and lady of Storn," he said. "You have told me of your fathers and how Horn became ruler, but tell me this: Is there not one of you who is not one of you?"

"Yes," said Sif. "Mouse! You mean Mouse!"

"The little one?" asked Ragnald, but it was not really a question. He knew whom she meant. "Your sister, Sigurd?"

"She's not really his sister," said Sif.

"Be quiet, Sif," I said angrily, but something bothered me.

"How do you know about Mouse?" I asked.

"I have had little to do since I have been here except to talk and to learn. And I have learned much, you see. If only I had my box, my special box, then I'd have something to do. Then I could keep your fathers busy, and all the rest of you, too. Oh, how you would dance to my tune!"

"But there's nothing in the box!" cried Sif. I had been about to say the same thing, and then I remembered that we weren't supposed to have even heard of the thing, let alone know where it was.

"Oh," said Sif, realizing what she had done.

"Oh," said Ragnald. "Oh. Yes. I know you have the box."

Sif nodded dumbly. I watched silently.

"And you are wrong," Ragnald continued. "There is *magic* in the box." He took a pendant from around his neck—it was shiny and gold and had a design of a horse's head on it. He rubbed it between his fingers as he spoke. I remember moonlight flashing off its shiny surface and flickering across my eyes. I turned my face and saw the same pale light play across Sif's face, too.

"Tell me something, wise ones," said Ragnald slowly. "Have you seen this marvelous box of mine? I know Horn says you haven't, but perhaps he is mistaken?"

I felt confused, as though there were something I had to do

but couldn't remember what. I looked to Sif for help, but she was staring straight at Ragnald.

"If only I knew where my box was," Ragnald went on steadily. "If only—then I could show you something unbelievable."

He stopped.

Sif turned her head to me, as if in a dream. There was no expression on her face. I said nothing, I remember, because I felt nothing.

"Yes," said Sif softly. "I know where it is. Come with me and show us your magic."

And Ragnald said, "Good."

That was how it started. Ragnald had shoved the boulder from the top of the hill. Unstoppable.

36

The darkness and smell of the kennel would have made Mouse feel truly at rest at any other time. The bitch, Moss, breathed gently next to her; Mouse felt her own breathing settle into rhythm with that of the dog. On another occasion she would quickly have settled into comfortable sleep, happy to lie there all night. But not now, because something was eating at her. She wanted to know where Sigurd was. No, the feeling was stronger than that. She had to find him.

Through Moss she heard all the minute sounds of the Storn that were beyond human hearing. She could hear the clank of beer mugs in the great broch. She listened harder and could hear someone snoring in his broch, and farther than that, Gudrun talking in her sleep in her hut.

Mouse listened on, directing her thoughts around the village, and then she heard something that made her blood run cold. From somewhere very close to Horn's broch she heard a voice she could not place.

"A single word from either of you and I'll slit your throats."

Mouse scrambled out of the kennel and ran.

37

We stood in the dark for a long time, just outside Horn's broch. In all that time it never entered my head to think we were doing something strange, so strange that it had to be crazy.

We could sense Horn inside, brooding. He must have left the great broch and come straight back. We wondered whether he would ever come out.

Eventually, after a long wait during which neither Ragnald nor Sif nor I said anything, someone, I do not to this day know who, approached the broch in the shadows.

The figure knocked on the lintel and went in. There were some words spoken, and then they left together, heading for the great broch.

We crept inside.

Only then did Ragnald speak.

"Where's the box?" he whispered at Sif.

She hesitated. She seemed half asleep.

"You want to see the magic, don't you?" Ragnald whispered again. "Where is it?"

"Oh," said Sif. "Yes."

She rummaged under some furs that lay against a wall. She pulled the box out from the furs.

"Here," she said.

It looked even more beautiful than I remembered.

"What sort of magic will it do, Ragnald?" I asked. I swear I had completely forgotten that we knew it was empty. That was just one more of Ragnald's games.

"The powerful sort," he said. He turned to Sif. "Give me the box."

She did as he told her.

"Now sit with your backs to the pole," he said, nodding at the tree trunk that ran to the center of the roof.

And we did.

"Now shut your eyes," he said.

And we did.

And the next thing I felt was a cord pulled hard around my throat. I jerked my head forward, but he was too quick. We sat back to back, with the cord round our throats and the pole, so tight we could not squeak, let alone speak. In the time it took us to try to pull the cord away with our hands, he had our arms tied fast by the elbows.

He took a long, double-edged knife from his bag.

I remember—how could I forget? I will remember the words he said next till the day I die.

"A single word from either of you and I'll slit your throats."

38

Mouse ran, not knowing what was wrong, what was happening, nor who was in danger. But she knew there was danger right in the very heart of the Storn.

She headed for the great broch; she could see lights burning inside in spite of the late hour. Her eyes were wide, but in fear she saw nothing and ran straight into someone in the dark.

She lost her footing and fell on the ground wildly.

"Princess?" said a voice.

"Who is it?" cried Mouse. "Who are you?"

"Are you hurt?"

"No," said Mouse. "Who is it?"

"Ragnald, my lady," said the voice. "Shall I help you to your feet?"

Mouse tried to stand and found herself pulled upright by a large, powerful hand.

"You are in a hurry, Lady?"

The tone of Ragnald's voice slowed Mouse. She could see him now, set against the silver moonlit sky.

"Yes," she said. She paused. "No, I . . ."

"Would you have a moment?" said Ragnald. "I have something to show you."

"No," said Mouse. "I mean, there is something—"

"It will take but a moment," said Ragnald. "And there is no one else. It is just for you, this thing."

"For me?" asked Mouse, and for a moment she forgot about finding Sigurd. "Are you sure?"

"Yes," said Ragnald, and he pulled the box from under his arm.

39

Oh, what fools we were!

I think something changed between us then.

As Sif and I sat, struggling for air because of the cord around our throats, unable to speak, I think we realized that no matter how much we disliked each other, we were going to have to think quickly if we wanted to live.

And then! What was he doing? The stranger . . . out in the darkness of the village, reunited with his magic.

Sif made a noise; I could tell only the emotion, not the meaning.

Fear. She was scared, and so was I.

The air was harder to pull into our lungs; the cord bit like fire into our throats.

Fire! A small chance, but it worked. With my left foot I was able to scrape a burning branch from Horn's fire. It went out as it rolled onto the earth floor, but the tip was still smoldering hot. I pulled it over to where we sat tied against the roof tree.

I could not pick it up, my hands were too tightly bound, but Sif, craning her head around, saw what I was trying to do. She picked the branch up with just her fingertips and managed to raise the other end of it, red-hot, into the air. The point wavered for a moment as she tried to steady the branch, but it was hard to hold. In desperation she let the smoldering point fall against the cord around our necks. It fell at a point midway between us, by the pole, and began to burn the cord, but instantly our skin began to burn, too.

We both screamed silently against the tightness of the cord, but in a few seconds the rope had weakened, and our jerks of pain snapped us free. With one end of the cord broken, we were able to wriggle free of our bonds quickly.

We both pressed our hands to the burns already seeping on our necks.

"Come on," I said, trying to get off my knees.

"I can't," said Sif, choking against the pain.

"We have to find him!" I cried.

She nodded.

"All right," she gasped. "All . . . right."

She staggered to her feet.

We stumbled out into the darkness. The cold wind felt good against the screaming, burning pain.

"What do we do? Where is he?" Sif cried

I felt I might panic. I tried to think calmly, to decide what was the best thing to do. "You go to the great broch. Get as much help as you can!" I said.

Immediately she ran toward the great broch.

There she would find Olaf and Thorbjorn, and as fate had it, Horn, too.

"I'll start looking for him," I called after her.

I think I sounded braver than I felt.

I looked around in the darkness.

Where was Ragnald?

We didn't even know what he was doing. I just knew it was something terrible. It had to be, to attack us so brutally, so coldly.

He had some purpose; I did not know what, but it was my belief it involved Mouse.

I was right, though it was the others who found her first.

40

When Horn and Olaf and Thorbjorn and Sif burst into the grain barn, they did not understand what they saw there. They did not understand what they saw, but it looked like evil.

By the dim light of a small candle they saw Mouse and the stranger, Ragnald.

Mouse was on her knees, writhing like a sick dog. Her feet scrabbled in the grain and dust, but her arms were rigid. Each of her hands was placed palm down against the inside of one half of the box, which was being held by Ragnald. Mouse's hands were held fast, as thought they were stuck to the inside of the box.

Ragnald stood above her, holding the box, whispering unknown words. Mouse was sobbing, her eyes closed, her body trembling.

"What is this?" Horn yelled as they broke in.

For just a moment there was a strange pause as each side regarded the other. Ragnald looked irritated for a moment, but then a smile spread across his face.

"So," he said, dropping the box.

Mouse fell beside it in the dirt, moaning as if in pain.

Ragnald pulled his long, toothed knife from his belt.

"So!" Horn said, and stepped forward with intent.

But as he drew his sword he remembered that all he had was the broken stump of Cold Lightning.

He looked at it blankly, and as he did so Ragnald took the chance to cut his throat.

Sif screamed.

Olaf stepped forward. He had come unarmed. They had not expected this. Ragnald opened Olaf's belly with a single sweep of his knife, and Olaf fell dying in the dirt.

Thorbjorn, who had a moment to gather his wits, shoved the burning flare he was carrying at the stranger's face, but Ragnald was fast and sidestepped. The torch fell to the ground.

"Ha!" he cried.

He stepped past the burning brand and circled Thorbjorn until his back was to the door of the barn.

He grinned and advanced on the now defenseless Thorbjorn.

Then there was a slight scuffling, the sound of someone entering the barn.

Ragnald began to turn, but before his face was even half toward the light, he was dead.

He slumped forward on the ground, falling onto the flare, putting out its light.

Behind him Sigurd knelt, staring at the broken stump of Horn's sword, which he had thrust into the stranger.

So, in about six seconds, it was over.

Part Two

THE DARK HORSE

1

To accord Horn the honor due him as Lawspeaker, we left his body on the hillside for the crows to eat.

My father was not so lucky—we buried his body under a single slab of rock on the low hills behind the village.

The death of a Lawspeaker is never a simple matter, but things were more complicated than normal. There was no obvious successor to Horn, just as there hadn't been when he and my father fought. The difference was that no one really wanted the job this time. No man, that is.

But before the tribe could even think of these things, there was the business of the departing dead to see to.

We took Horn's body on a wooden stretcher to the circle of rock fingers on the hill above the bay, known as Bird Rock. Everyone went, as is the law. Even Gudrun managed to walk up the hill—her first journey outside the village since her accident.

Mouse walked next to me. I remember she was silent, so

silent. Perhaps I should have realized then that something serious had changed in her. Something had happened to her when Ragnald had . . . what? I'm still not sure what he did to her, but he had changed her somehow.

She had never been loud, but now she was quieter than ever. If it had been possible, I would have said she was even quieter than when she first came to us. But I did not realize this fully, my mind empty; I felt little. It was all a dream to me, just as it seems to me now, looking back after all these years.

I suppose something of me died with my father. That seems likely, doesn't it? Maybe that was why I felt nothing as we walked up the cold hillside.

But Sif cried. I remember that well. I remember being a little surprised by it. I should not have been.

We put Horn's body on the stone table in the center of the circle, and Gudrun said some words. I do not remember them.

Then Longshank spoke.

"This place is now sacrosanct. It is forbidden to return to Bird Rock until the new Lawspeaker, whoever he may be, returns to light the bone fire."

Not that anyone ever went up there anyway, except Gudrun, and, I think, Mouse.

Then we left Horn on Bird Rock for the crows to come and clean his bones.

I was not sorry to leave, for my mother and I had our own duties to perform before the day was done.

Once we were back in the village, my mother, keeping her dignity as well as she could, asked two or three of the men to help us. I didn't really notice who.

We carried Olaf out to the low hill where we buried people. We dug a shallow trench; it was only a foot or two to the bedrock, and then we put Father into the hole. On top we laid the biggest slab of rock we could move, so that people would know there was someone buried underneath.

Then the men left, silently, and Mouse, Mother, and I stood around for a while, thinking our own things.

Mouse, silent since Ragnald had attacked her, finally made a sound. But not exactly a human one.

She whimpered, like an injured dog.

Freya put a hand on her shoulder.

"Shush," she said gently, and Mouse grew silent again.

Then we returned to the village.

That was how we sent my father on his way to the next world.

"What will happen now?" I asked as we walked back.

Mother shook her head.

"I don't know," she said.

2

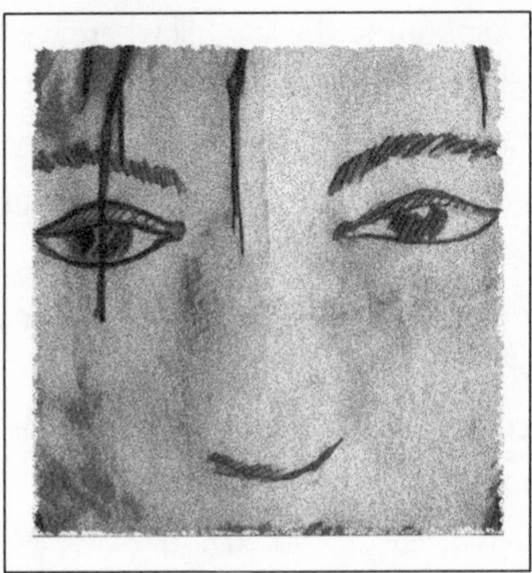

Longshank peered through the murk of smoke inside the great broch. The faces of the whole village stared back at him.

Everyone awaited the result of his deliberation over the law.

"Upon the death of the Lawspeaker," he said, "the position shall be filled by the Lawspeaker's son."

There was a murmur.

Mouse saw Sif stare angrily through the fire.

"But Horn has no son," Longshank continued, "in which case the position shall fall to his nearest male relative."

There was another murmur.

"But Horn has no living male relative," said Longshank.

"We know!" cried a voice from the back of the broch.

Longshank jerked his head round to stare at the place the voice had come from.

"Get on with it!" called out another voice.

"Very well," Longshank said. "In this case the position returns to the last person to contest the fight with the dead Lawspeaker, unless anyone wishes to challenge *that* person to a trial."

This had been the case with Olaf and Horn, but there was a further problem: Olaf had perished at Ragnald's hand.

"But," said Longshank, "since the challenger is no longer alive, either, the position falls to his son."

There was a huge uproar in the broch.

"So," said Longshank, though no one listened to him because they already knew what it meant, "the boy Sigurd shall be pronounced Lawspeaker, provided he passes his coming-of-age trial."

The tumult continued.

Sigurd stared wildly about him. Why had no one told him this was possible? Surely someone other than Longshank knew the law.

Mouse felt her heart quicken.

Sif jumped to her feet.

The room quieted a little.

"Assuming," said Longshank, taking the opportunity to finish, "that no one wishes to challenge the boy?"

He looked around the room, at all the grown men who had grumbled about Horn and about how he had ruled. But they all were quiet.

"No one challenges?" asked Longshank scornfully.

"Yes! I do!"

Everyone turned and stared at Sif.

"Yes," she cried, "I do!"

3

And so we fought. Sif and I. No one could stop her; no one could challenge her right to fight me for the position of Lawspeaker. Though a few people tried to point out that she was a girl and that a girl could not be Lawspeaker, Longshank had to admit that this was not actually recorded in the law. It was no more than tradition.

And me?

After the shock, the shock of finding out I would be Lawspeaker, a desire began to grow in me.

It grew rapidly, and as I thought about my father, my *dead* father, and Horn, it grew even more. A desire to shake this tribe of stupid men and make something of them, despite it all.

So when Sif insisted, as the days passed, that she wanted to fight me, and as all the strong men of the village stared at me when I walked by, I became more and more determined to take her on.

Mouse didn't want me to do it. I couldn't find out exactly why she was so against it.

"Why?" she asked again and again.

I would look at her and shrug.

"No one else wants to do it," I would say weakly.

But there was more to it than that.

"Why don't you want me to?" I asked her.

Now it was her turn to be evasive.

"You said you'd be my brother," she said. "Always."

"But I'll still be your brother," I protested.

"You'll be Lawspeaker," she said, and then, when I pressed her, "There is danger with it."

But she would say no more.

But before Sif and I fought, there was more disposing of dead to be done.

Ragnald's body had lain under some sacking in the grain store, where he had fallen with Horn's broken blade in his back. The sword that I had put there. Now it was time to do something about it.

This reminds me that a strange thing had happened when we covered Ragnald's body with the sacking.

For the first time since Ragnald's attack, I thought about the box. We had left it lying on the floor of the grain barn, where it had fallen from the stranger's hands. It filled me with fear, and I wanted, if it was possible, to destroy it. It seemed to me that it must be full of evil magic. But while Freya was covering Ragnald's body, I looked for the box. It was gone. I asked round the village, but no one claimed to have it.

And I seemed to be the only one bothered by this.

"A piece of magic like that," people said, "so strong. It will have died with its owner. It must have vanished when Ragnald perished."

I forgot about it; there was other work to do.

It was decided that the most fitting fate for a stranger who had come to try to harm us was to feed his body to the fish. So we prepared to take Ragnald's body out into the bay in a boat.

An interesting thing had started to happen. Since it had been announced that I might be Lawspeaker, people had taken more notice of me. And of Freya and Mouse, too. But mostly of me.

Maybe because I had been the one to stick the sword into Ragnald. Maybe that had made people take notice of me. I had displayed bravery and strength, and those things were supposed to be important to us.

And now the men who had supported my father and me stood around and asked me what to do, while those who had ridiculed him seemed lost. As indeed they were, leaderless without Horn. There was no way these men would support Sif, a girl, in her claim to be Lawspeaker.

"Roll him up in the cloth," I said, pointing at Ragnald's corpse, "and get him into the boat. We don't want his ghost haunting us here. The sooner the fish pick his bones clean, the better for all of us."

And everyone agreed. He was obviously some kind of magician; he would be more likely than most to prove a troublesome spirit after death.

Mouse stood and watched with me as the men went about

the work. We hadn't spoken of that awful night since it had happened. Now I could not restrain my curiosity.

"What did he do to you?" I asked. "With the box—what was he doing?"

Mouse looked at me in her silent way.

"He hurt me," she said in the voice that meant I would get no more out of her.

So we put Ragnald into the boat, rowed out to the waiting sea, and tipped him overboard.

4

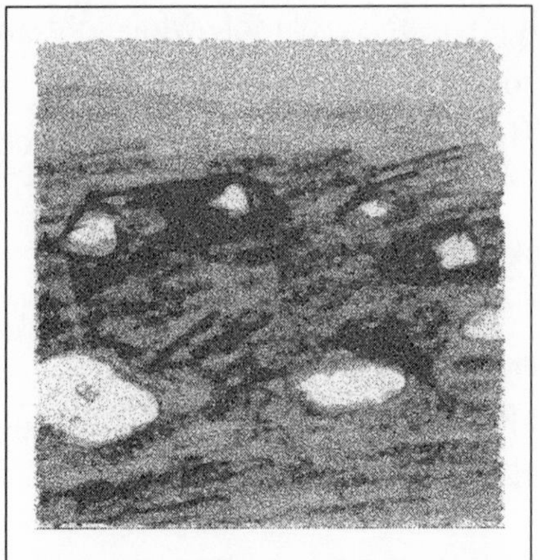

"Sigurd Olafsson!" called Longshank.

"Yes," the boy answered.

"Sif Hornsdaughter!" called the old man again.

"Yes," answered the girl.

The pair stood opposite each other in a crudely marked circle of white pebbles on the black beach. The tribe watched from the high-tide line. Mouse held Freya's hand. She didn't know which of them was comforting the other.

Sif had continued to insist that she go through with her challenge to Sigurd's right to become Lawspeaker.

"You know why you are here? You know the rules by which you must abide?" asked Longshank.

"Yes," answered boy and girl together.

"Then begin!"

But the fight was over almost as soon as it started.

Sif was a tall, strong girl, but at sixteen Sigurd was bigger and stronger than some men ten years older.

She made the first move and charged at Sigurd, screaming loudly.

She made an impressive sight, and for a moment Sigurd was thrown by her aggression.

As she reached him he recovered himself, bouncing his body weight into his knees. A moment before she would have struck him, he shifted onto his left foot, and Sif flew past. As she did so he swung into her stomach with a tight fist.

Sif lay sprawling, winded, on the sand. Sigurd put his foot on her throat.

"Yield," he said, but quietly and without show.

Sif tried to wriggle out, but Sigurd put more weight on her.

"Yield," he said again, and then whispered so that no one at the beach could hear, "Your father would be proud."

Sif stopped wriggling. After a long pause she raised a hand in submission.

A murmur came from the watching crowd.

Sif stood and glared at Sigurd, her nose just a few inches from his. Then she spat in his face and walked back to the brochs, her rage still twisting inside her.

Sigurd followed more slowly, and behind him walked Longshank, with due solemnity.

As Sigurd reached the people Longshank called out, "Hail to the new Lawspeaker!"

There was a shout, but it was subdued. As if for the first time, what was happening was sinking into everyone's mind.

Sigurd met every gaze as he walked through the tribe, which parted to let him into his village.

All was total silence, apart from the whisk of the wind coming off the sea. Then a woman's voice muttered, "Are we really to be ruled by a boy?"

Sigurd stopped in his tracks. He looked about him for the source of the voice.

"Yes," he said. "Since no man is bold enough, you will be ruled by a boy."

No one spoke.

Evening fell.

Inside his broch, with all the people hidden in their own dark homes, Sigurd shook and cried like a small child while Freya held him tight.

Mouse sat at his feet, quiet.

"Your father would be proud," said Freya again.

5

Then Longshank decided that I should undergo my coming-of-age ordeal. In this way, he said, I would become a man, so the tribe would have a man for Lawspeaker after all, and not a boy.

I was not afraid either way. I wanted to do it.

So the morning after I had defeated Sif in the fight, they set up the arch made of turf on the grass between the village and the fields.

To complete the ordeal, all I had to do was walk under the arch. If it fell down while I did so, then my manhood would be a poor affair. If not, then I would prosper.

I walked under the low arch made of a single thick sod of grass curved up into the air. It held, and it was over.

I raised my hands.

"What now, Lawspeaker?" asked Longshank.

I remember how strange it felt to be called by my title.
I pointed at Bird Rock.
"To the hill," I said. "We have bones to burn."
We went to make the bone fire.

6

Dusk on Bird Rock.

All day under Sigurd's direction the village had dragged long, neat logs up to the top of the hill to the circle of rock fingers. Now night had started to fall, and they would have liked to be safely back in the village. But there was work to be done still; the final episode in Horn's life.

Their first arrival at the site had not been pleasant.

Horn's body was not what it had been. The crows had been at their work and had stripped much flesh from the bones, but they had worked messily. The picked and pulled remains of Horn lay both on and around the central table rock of the circle.

In theory the body should have been left until the bones were clean, but in practice that never happened.

So Sigurd directed men twice his age and more to build a funeral pyre around the base of the table rock. It was a massive pyre, but it would take a lot of heat to burn the bones.

It would also take all night.

As night fell a select few of the villagers gathered around the stack of wood and bone.

There was Sigurd, obviously. Sif was there. She was silent. She neither spoke nor even met anyone's gaze. Gudrun, who had come up at dusk, hovered first near Sigurd, then near Sif, then withdrew to the shadows. She waited while the final preparations were made. There was Herda, to sing a lament, and Longshank, to instruct in the procedure. There were one or two who had been Horn's favorites.

Finally all was ready.

"Do it, then," said a weary voice.

"Yes," said Sigurd, and he shoved a firebrand into the base of the wood.

Before long the fire crackled and flames leaped up into the air around the circle.

Gudrun stepped forward and began to say final words for Horn.

Night fell, and the small group watched the fire, till one by one they fell asleep. In the morning the breeze would blow the ashes into the air, and Horn's life would have been properly respected.

7

They were strange times, those first days after I became Lawspeaker. The world moved like a dream that I was watching, and not even my own dream. It seemed like someone else's life that I was stealing a part in.

We sat at the top of the hill and watched Horn's bones burn.

Longshank fell asleep first. Then Herda.

Sif and I watched each other across the fire, brooding on our own thoughts. Then she fell asleep, too.

I was alone at the top of Bird Rock. All other minds had left me.

And then Mouse appeared.

I wasn't aware of her coming. But then she was beside me.

"Mouse," I said, "you shouldn't be here."

"Are you going to make me go away, Lawspeaker?" she asked.

I was silent.

"No," I said after a while. "No, of course not."

We sat there in silence for a long time. I think I fell asleep. I know I did, because I woke to witness the beginning of the storm.

8

Mouse sat with eyes staring past the bone fire, out to the sea. She alone was awake, all the others having long ago drifted to sleep, even Sigurd.

She looked at her brother, and fear began to grow in her. She did not know why, but something about the firelit scene before her nagged at her memory.

For Mouse, memory was something to be feared, something not to be trusted. She could remember her life with the Storn, and she could remember the time with the wolves, though she had forgotten some. Besides, she didn't like remembering that time—it only brought pain. The pain that comes with loss.

Of the time that lay before that, she could remember nothing. But now, sitting on the hill, only an eyelid's distance away from sleep, she recognized something. People huddled outside around a fire. A hillside that overlooked the sea but that rolled away to high plains inland. Away in the woods of the valleys a wolf hunted. Around her feet a shrew scrabbled in the scrubby grass at the base of one of the stone fingers.

Above her head an eagle owl whirled. From its position on high it saw the humans' fire and came to have a closer look. With its powerful eyesight it saw the movement of the shrew and plummeted groundward. Only at the last second, though, did it see Mouse, hidden and still by the rock. The owl hesitated in its descent, and the shrew disappeared into its hole.

The owl wheeled away and out to sea.

Then there was the sea itself, and the wind, and the sound of horses stamping their feet, pulling at their tethers.

They're coming.

They're coming.

Horses? Now Mouse knew she had been dreaming, and indeed as she opened her eyes daybreak had come.

As she shook her head free of sleep the disturbing images from the night would not leave her entirely.

"They're coming," she murmured.

"Hmm?" said Sigurd, waking slowly beside her.

But Mouse said nothing because she didn't know what she meant.

Other people woke now, and stood and stretched. The fire was smoldering gently, but it had done its job—there was no trace of the old Lawspeaker left. All was ashes, which were gradually being swept into the air by the stiffening breeze.

Then Mouse saw the boat.

She pointed down to the shore.

"A merchant ship!" said Herda.

Sigurd looked round. Merchants. He needed to be in the village. He believed Horn had traded poorly with these men. That had to change if they were to survive.

"Quickly," he said. Without any further ceremony they all left Bird Rock. All except Sif.

9

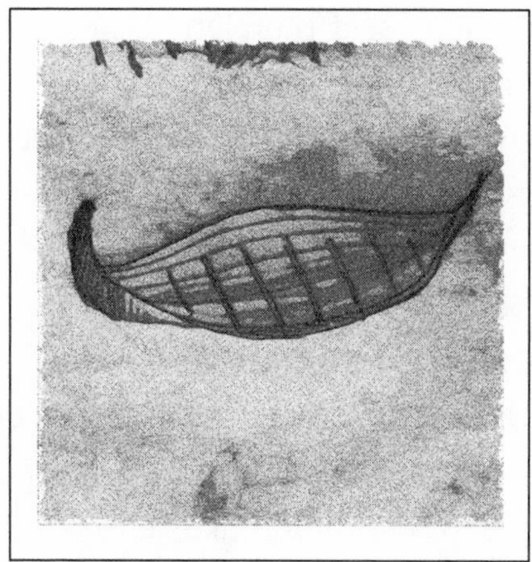

By the time we made it down from the hill, much of the rest of the Storn had almost completely encircled the trading ship, which lay beached on the shore. The boat was a knorr—one of those small, open-decked seagoing boats favored by merchantmen, for it could hold a big cargo for its size.

I could see its carved prow above the crowd. As I approached I began to realize that something was happening—there were many more people than usual gathered around the boat. And it was too quiet.

I pushed my way through from the back of the circle of people. As I came into the middle I stopped dead.

In front of me were two or three of the traders. I recognized their leader from a previous visit, though I couldn't remember his name.

"So this is the new Lawspeaker," he said as I arrived. But I paid him no attention because I saw the body at his feet straightaway.

"They found him," said Thorbjorn. "They found him in the shallows farther down the coast."

"He's come back!" someone else cried hysterically.

"Who?" I asked. "Who is it?"

"We thought he might be one of yours," said the merchant, and rolled the body over with his foot.

I should have recognized him sooner.

Ragnald. Or what was left of him after two days of bobbing around in the sea. Even though his face was disfigured, his white hair and black palms were unmistakable.

"He's not yours?" asked the trader.

"No," I said quietly.

I felt what we were all feeling. It was an omen.

10

"You brought him here. You take him back!"

Sigurd stared straight at the merchant.

His name was Morten, and if he thought his job would be even easier now that the fool called Horn had been replaced by a boy, he was wrong. Sigurd sat opposite Morten, who was flanked by a pair of his men. Around the new Lawspeaker sat his chosen advisers, Thorbjorn, so large and strong, and Herda, so gentle and wise. Sigurd met Morten's gaze and would not back down, though his heart beat hard in his chest.

"You admit you put this man in the sea," Morten stated. He was a short, stout man. He didn't look like a sailor, but he was obviously a very successful trader.

Sigurd nodded. "That much is true."

"And the sea has brought him back to you. You cannot ignore this fact."

"The sea brought him back to land—you brought him back to us."

Again Sigurd stared at the man, until finally Morten's face broke into a smile.

"Very well," he laughed. "I can see you are determined. We will take him far out to sea with us when we leave, and finish what you started."

Sigurd nodded.

"Thank you," he said.

"And in return for this, I am sure you will want to help us?"

Morten smiled at the boy in front of him.

Sigurd heard some whispering around him. He put up his hand.

"Let us hear what Morten the trader has to say," he said.

Morten took a long drink from the beer mug in his hand before he spoke.

"Times are hard," he said. "We have fared badly on our current expedition. Every tribe of every village has traded poorly with us. Crops have failed along the entire length of coast that we have sailed. Our boat is still full of the things we brought to barter with when we set out four months ago. Our coffers are empty of silver."

"I can imagine," said Sigurd. "What of it?"

"Lawspeaker, in order that we return home not entirely empty-handed, we simply ask you to consider our wares and the reasonable price we will accept for them. We are sure that this tribe has not sunk as low as others we have seen, which cannot afford a few luxuries for themselves."

"And what would you have us give you in return?" Sigurd asked. "In return for these luxuries? Our grain is nearly all gone. This year's crop is dying in the fields. We have no fish to spare; we cannot catch enough to feed ourselves. We have nothing of value to barter with."

Some of the men muttered behind him.

"It is wrong to speak of the Storn that way," said Thorbjorn.

Sigurd turned to him. "No. Those days are past. We must face the truth now. We are in trouble, and the truth is that we are so poor that we have nothing to offer Morten and his men. We must face this truth, or we will die before we even know why."

There was silence.

Morten smiled at Sigurd again, but it was a grim smile this time.

"I can see the new Lawspeaker will give the tribe the best chance of survival he can."

He stood up.

"Come," he said to his men. "We go."

Sigurd rose to face him. "Already? You are still welcome to stay with us for a few days. We do not have much, but we will share our hospitality with you until you are rested. That is the custom."

"Custom?" said Morten. "The days for custom may be at an end. We have no desire to stay anywhere longer than is necessary for trade."

Morten turned to leave, then stopped and spoke again.

"I will tell you this. You have impressed me with your courage, Lawspeaker, but I fear that will not be enough to save you."

"With prudence we will outlive this famine," said Sigurd, but Morten laughed bitterly.

"I am not speaking of the hunger," he said. "We have sailed far to the north this time. If you think your life is hard here, it is much worse there. Brochs lie empty. Whole villages are deserted—the people either dead or gone. And not because of the famine."

"Then why?"

"The Dark Horse," said Morten quietly.

His words fell like stones into a still pool. And just like the ripples spreading across that pool, the fear spread through them all.

Sigurd turned to Thorbjorn, who dropped his eyes to the floor. Seeing the big man scared unnerved Sigurd badly.

Morten spoke once more.

"We did not see them ourselves, but many places we went had been visited by them. We spoke to one or two people whom they missed. It seems they are suffering, too. The herds they follow are dwindling. They are heading south instead, looking for easier pickings. No one can stop them. My advice to you is to run."

He turned again.

"Come. To the boat," he called to his men. He swept out of the broch and down to the shore.

"And where shall we run?" cried Sigurd, following him out of the broch.

Morten answered without even looking around.

"They're coming," was all he said. "They're coming."

11

So then the gray sky grew black above our heads.

The Dark Horse.

Of course we had all heard of them, but I think many people doubted that they even existed. They were like a legend, like something from a story, and I suppose no one liked to think about them any more than that, for they were death.

Fearsome horsemen, they were fabled to live a very different life from our own peaceful existence of farming and fishing. They were supposed to follow the herds of deer across the dark coldness of the far north. Living in great tents, they could pack their entire village in a night and move on at the speed of a galloping horse.

As Morten hurriedly prepared for sea, the rumor that he had started had already spread around the whole village. There were shouting and crying. It was terrible.

Freya, my good mother, stood next to me as we watched them load Ragnald's body back on board. They promised to drop him far out to sea, but I was sure I saw them slip something overboard before they had even disappeared round the headland of the bay.

"What have I done?" I asked Freya after the ship was out of sight.

"What do you mean?" she asked.

"I should have let a man become Lawspeaker. How can I save us if the Dark Horse come?"

"They all had their chance," she said. "You are the best man here. You will see us safe. Take courage from your name."

I must have looked confused.

"Your name," she said. "Have I never told you what it means?"

I shook my head.

"Sigurd. 'The peace that comes with victory.' You see, you cannot fail!"

And despite everything, she laughed.

I remember wishing that what she had said would be true.

12

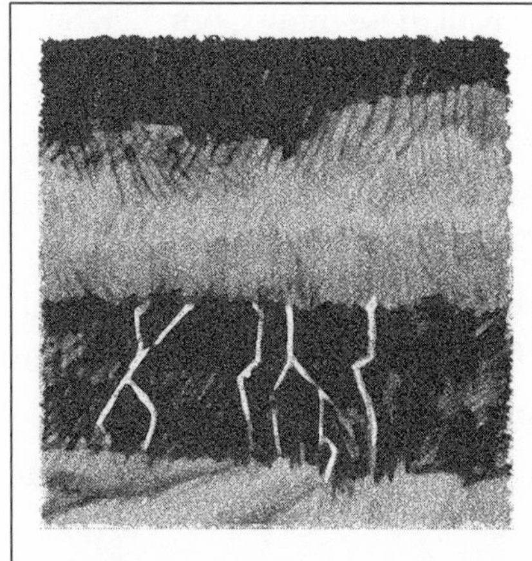

That night there was a meeting in the great broch.

Sigurd's style of leadership was very different from Horn's. All Horn's discussions and decisions had been made with two or three of his cronies in his own broch. Now Sigurd had been given the Lawspeaker's broch as his own, but he chose instead to call the entire village into the great broch to hear what he had to say.

But things were not to happen as he expected.

He told them that it was true, that Morten the trader had said the Dark Horse were riding south.

He told them that if this was true, there was nothing they could do to stop it.

He told them that all they could do was prepare to fight if they had to.

He told them last that if they did not ration their food and work hard at fishing and in the fields, then they would starve long before the Dark Horse got anywhere near them.

He told them all these things, but then Sif stood and challenged him.

"Why are we listening to this?" she demanded. "If we stay here, we will die. We will either starve or be killed. I say we should go now."

"Where would you go, Sif?" asked Sigurd.

"Where? That does not matter! I say we should go. I am Horn's daughter, and I say we should go!"

Sigurd was silent while he tried to judge the mood of the people.

No one said anything; many gazed at the floor, avoiding Sigurd's gaze.

Then Sif spoke again, angrier this time.

"Are you all fools?" she cried. "Are you going to sit here and die? I say we should go, and I am leaving! Who will come with me? Who will come with me?"

She looked around the hall. There was no movement.

She approached some of the men who had been her father's favorites.

"In the name of my father, will you not stir yourselves and follow me?"

"Sit down, Sif," said Longshank.

Sif whirled around.

"Do you doubt me?" she screamed. "Very well! I am leaving. Tonight! And anyone who is not stupid will come with me. A curse on the rest of you!"

And she left the hall in a fury.

And thus she left the tribe.

13

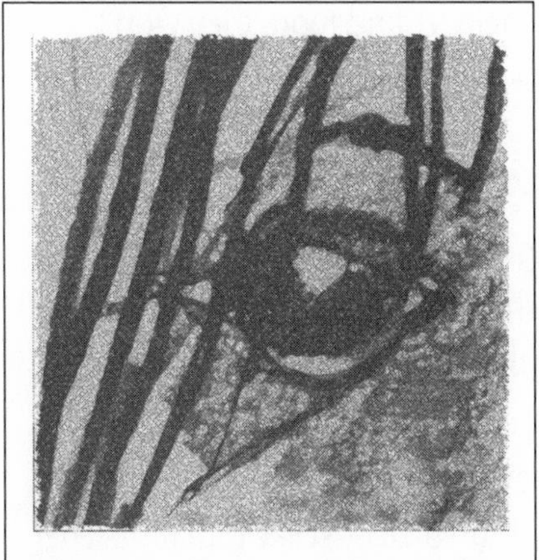

Sif could not be persuaded to stay.

She had always been stubborn, and this case was like many that had gone before. The difference was that she left, by herself, for who knows where. I myself did not mourn her going—there was too much else to worry about. Food, for a start.

I had decided that there was something we could do about the situation, something we could have done before. We had a powerful thing that we could have been using to help us, instead of ignoring or fearing.

"I need your help, Mouse," I said as we climbed the low hills behind the village. It was the morning after Sif had left.

"What?" she asked.

"We could use your help. The whole village, you could help us all. You could find us food. Just like you did that time with the fish, remember?"

"They hated me for that."

"They feared you. They didn't hate you. . . . And now they're hungry. If you help us find food, they won't care how you did it. They'll be too grateful to care."

"People . . . ," she began, but trailed off.

"So, what?" I asked.

She shrugged.

"Selfish," she said, but she sounded as if she didn't really know whether that was the right word.

"Maybe," I said, "but these are our people."

She said nothing.

"I know you can do it. Just like that time when you showed us where the fish were."

Mouse said nothing. I tried to encourage her.

"How did you do it?" I asked.

"The birds were calling to one another," she said. "I felt them telling one another where to fish."

The way she said it made it sound so simple.

"But you could do it again?" I asked, though I knew the answer. I suspected Mouse was probably capable of a lot more than we knew.

"Yes," she said.

"So you'll help?" I asked. "Leave the Storn to me."

She nodded, but she looked doubtful.

It was a start, at least.

14

Mouse did as Sigurd Lawspeaker had asked, but only after Gudrun had spoken to the girl, too.

"Don't tell me you've saved my life only to let me starve?" said the Wisewoman with a smile on her face, and at last Mouse was persuaded.

A really good catch of fish would go a long way. Anything they did not eat fresh could be smoked and dried to eat later. Then all Sigurd had to do was make sure crops did not perish.

Sigurd had said she could use his broch to work her magic, but she had refused the offer.

"It's easier outside, closer to the world."

He had nodded, and she had wandered away, to find a quiet spot, he presumed.

In fact, she now lay staring at the sky from a point about halfway toward Bird Rock.

It was early morning. She sat and watched the sun begin

to shine over the sea horizon, bringing the blue to life from the gray water.

A bird.

Where?

There. That was what she needed. A sea-fishing bird. A flight of cormorants clung to a cliffside away and up to her right.

She waited, finding a mind to attach herself to.

With a suddenness that almost frightened her she was leaping from the cliff with one of the elegant black birds. The sea lay below her, rich and smooth from this height.

The bird folded its wings and arrowed at the sea surface. She plunged into the dark, freezing water with the bird. It was deafening and silent all at the same time. There was a lot of sound, but it made no sense. Just the rush of water as the bird struck a fish and wrestled it back to the surface.

But as the cormorant rose back to the light Mouse felt herself slipping out of it. There was something else there, something more powerful that was pulling her out of the mind of the bird.

The bird had gone, and Mouse was alone in the depths of the sea. She could see nothing, could hear nothing.

She could feel the cold of the water, but then something began to burn at her brain, demanding attention.

Slowly she was aware that she could see a light.

Firelight.

She didn't understand how it was possible, given that her mind was underwater, but there was definitely a fire in front of her. Before she had time to wonder any more, other shapes began to materialize around the fire.

Then it all snapped into focus.

She lay still, in a bed of furs. She could see people sitting around the fire, shapes and shadows moving on the ceiling above her.

Then the ceiling itself moved, and Mouse realized it was a patchwork of hides sewn into a huge domed tent. The smoke from the fire spiraled out of a small vent in the center of the circle that formed the roof, and she saw a star twinkling on the other side.

Outside she heard horses gently whinnying to one another. She longed to step into their minds, but then a voice spoke.

It was a voice from the fireside.

Mouse came tumbling out of the picture and felt herself hit the seabed. It was sandy, just pure sand, but then, as she tried to push herself back to the real world, her hands felt something soft. She thought it was seaweed, but as she looked she saw it was hair.

White hair.

She looked at Ragnald's decomposing body and screamed a scream, sea deep and silent.

She woke and ran from the hillside, tears streaming down her face.

15

I was so young then, and yet my heart was heavy.

I had assumed it would be an easy thing for her to lead us to plentiful fishing. But all she had found was the touchstone lurking in Ragnald's rotting body at the bottom of the sea.

It seemed we would never be rid of this man.

Mouse took a lot of calming when she came down from the hill. Mother and I sat with her for a long time while she spoke about the pictures she had seen.

We tried to reassure her, but if I were honest, I would say that I was scared by her words.

"They're coming," Morten had said.

With a sickening dread I wondered whether what Mouse had seen was Ragnald's own tribe.

Words came into my head: Have we had one of the Dark Horse in our midst and not realized it?

Then why had he come on foot?

It made little sense, but as I say, I felt that fate was working against me.

No fish.

The people complained but worked no harder.

Death had already come once.

I knew it would come again.

16

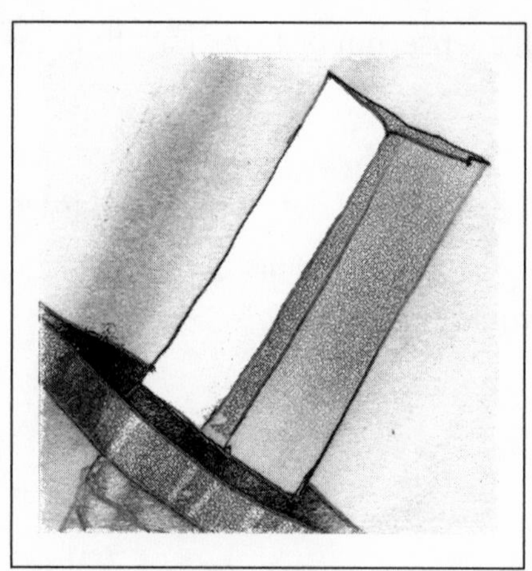

It was as if the years had fallen away, for Mouse became silent again, just as she had been when the Storn found her.

Whether it was from shock or fear, no one could tell, but she kept herself to herself and would speak to no one. Not even Sigurd.

She made use of all her old haunts—the grain store and the hills—and she began to sleep in the hounds' kennel house again. This time no one tried to stop her.

Evening.

There was yet another meeting in the great broch, and the Storn were, at last, roused to some passion. Everyone was there except Mouse.

Sigurd had a hard job to make himself heard, let alone obeyed. He could not understand what had changed them, at first. Something had changed, and soon Sigurd understood what had moved them.

Fear.

"People!" he cried above the tumult of voices raised in the hall. But he was not heeded.

"This will achieve nothing!" he cried again and again, but he could not be heard above the shouts and arguments that seemed to blame him for everything.

He looked desperately at his mother for inspiration, but Freya shook her head. She looked as scared as everyone else.

Sigurd gave up. He rose from his seat by the fire and started to walk to the door.

Amazingly, as he went, the room fell quiet, so that by the time he was at the threshold, there was absolute silence. He hadn't intended this, but it had worked.

Sigurd shook his head.

"Lawspeaker?" said Hemm, the dog handler.

All faces turned to Sigurd. Steadily he looked around the broch. He met every gaze, and as he did so each head dropped in shame. He walked slowly back into the center of the broch. He reached the fire. After a long time he finally spoke.

"So, this is the great tribe of the Storn. Reduced to an arguing rabble, with no respect for themselves or the law.... And what is to be done? Longshank, what would you do? Hemm, what about you?"

He looked from face to face, but there was no reply.

"We are scared, Sigurd," said Thorbjorn.

Sigurd nodded.

"I know," he said. He didn't add: And so am I.

"And is it true?" asked Hemm. "About the Dark Horse?"

Sigurd nodded again.

"I have made a mistake. I thought we needed to think about food first. I was wrong. We need to think about food and defending ourselves in equal measure. From tomorrow morning we will start to build a defensive ditch and wall around the village. But we will continue our work in the fields, and the fishing will continue as normal."

Now murmurs started again in the hall.

"How are we to do all this?" called a voice.

Sigurd peered into the gloom at the back of the hall.

"With hard work," he said. "With hard work and a determination to prevail.... And those of you who are not ready to try had better leave now. Follow Sif, wherever she has gone, and try your chances there. But the rest of us will stay here and make it work."

Sigurd stopped and waited, but there were no more complaints.

"Very well," he said. "Weapons. I want each man with a sword to raise his arm now."

About a quarter of the people present raised their arm.

Sigurd tried to quell the fear that rose in his throat.

"Anyone with a spear or other weapon, raise your hand."

A few more people put their hand in the air.

"Very well. Thorbjorn will be busy in the forge from tomorrow also."

"But we have little iron, Sigurd," said Thorbjorn.

"Do what you can," said Sigurd. "And get what help you need."

"I have not been idle," said Thorbjorn a little defensively. "Wait!"

He left the hall but returned a minute later with a long bundle of cloth.

He approached Sigurd.

"As you know, Cold Lightning could not be mended. But the Lawspeaker must not be without a sword."

Thorbjorn unwrapped the cloth. Out of it he pulled a gleaming, bright weapon. A fire-new sword. It was a good piece of work—Sigurd could tell that immediately.

"Forged from the broken pieces of Cold Lightning—the new Lawspeaker's sword!"

Thorbjorn held it high for everyone to see. It glimmered and glowed in the firelight, and a hush descended once more.

Sigurd took the piece in his hands.

"It shall be called Fire-fresh!" he cried.

And hope was not yet dead.

17

I went to see Mouse, to show her Fire-fresh, to see if that would shake her from her mute stillness.

I found her, for once, in her own home, the broch that she and I had shared with Father and Mother for many years.

She stared into the fire, and though I tried again to rouse her, she would not even look at me, let alone speak.

But it was all for nothing, for it was then that the world was ripped apart.

There were shouts outside. I ran to see what was happening.

Egil Hemmson, a boy just a few years younger than me, stood on the roof of the great broch. How he got there I do not know, but I will remember to my last day how he stood still and pointed.

He pointed to the hill horizon, up behind the village.

"Look!" he cried. "Look!"

People followed his gaze.

"What is it, boy?" shouted his father.

"Horsemen! Horsemen!"

We all looked, but there was nothing.

"Idiot boy! Get down!"

But then I saw, too.

"No," I said. "No. He's right. . . ."

For a long time we stared at the hill, and as the clouds came and went we saw the figures more clearly. A string of men on horseback strung out across the horizon.

All was calm; there was an unnatural quiet. We did nothing.

And then there was a scream.

"Horsemen! On the beach!"

"Quick!"

"To your arms!" I cried.

And it was true. All my talk of preparing ourselves. It was all for nothing because the Dark Horse had already come.

I don't know who spotted the second set of horsemen riding at us along the beach, but before we had time even to panic, we could hear the thundering of their horses' hooves as they attacked at full speed along the shoreline.

Even in the split second before they struck, there was time to think a thousand thoughts. But on top of all the simple things—like fear and wondering if there was any hope and trying to plan some kind of defense—one thing struck me. A thought that filled me with a sudden and profound horror.

The Dark Horse were so confident of victory that they could

leave half their number up on the hillside to watch. We would be slaughtered.

"To your arms!" I cried again.

Now there was total panic. I was torn. I wanted to find Mouse and Mother, but I was Lawspeaker now. I held Fire-fresh tightly in my fist and ran to gather our men to the front of the attack.

18

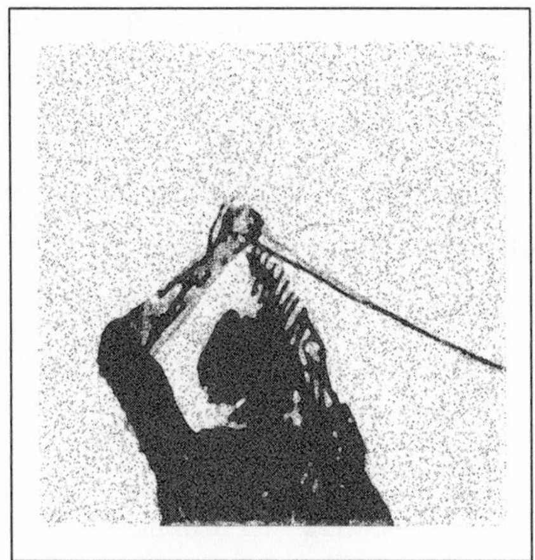

The Dark Horse spread fear before them—the sound of their horses' hoofbeats drummed louder and louder each second, until even the noise of the sea was silenced.

Sigurd gathered a dozen men around him at the edge of the village.

"Use the buildings!" he called. "Cover your backs!"

He had realized that out in the open they would be cut down as easily as the wheat at Harvest-month.

The crazy pattern of tiny brochs offered some protection from the horsemen. It was a small plan of sorts, but just a moment before the Dark Horse struck, there were more shouts from the village.

"They're coming from the other side!"

In the confusion that followed, the first wave of riders was upon them.

Instantly Sigurd could see that the situation was hopeless. They were a tribe of farmers and fishers, and not very good ones at that. They were being attacked by an army, a ruthless, specialized tribe of killers who had done this a hundred times before.

In the first few seconds many Storn men died of horse-borne spear thrusts. The black horses tore through the village, weaving their way expertly between the brochs.

A great screaming arose, and Sigurd saw that there was no hope. He watched with horror as Longshank fell easily under the blade of an ax.

The Dark Horse seemed to cut down two of the Storn with each swing of the sword. Sigurd hesitated a moment longer, but there was no doubt.

"All is lost!" he cried. "Run! Run for your lives!"

He ran wildly through the village, calling to everyone to flee. He found Freya, running toward him.

"Mother! Where's Mouse? We must get away!"

"She's in the broch. She won't come out!"

"I'll get her! You go! Take Skinfax and go!"

"Where are we going?"

"To the hills, tell everyone you can to run to the hills!"

And he went, leaving his mother to do the best she could.

Sigurd ran past the great broch to his old home.

He burst in and found Mouse.

She looked up at him as he came in.

"What is it?" she asked.

"Mouse! We must go! The Dark Horse . . . we must run!"

She shook her head. "No, Sigurd, I must stay."

"What! Why?"

She shrugged. "I must stay."

"No!" shouted Sigurd.

Mouse jumped at the ferocity of his voice.

"Come on! Now!"

She hesitated.

From outside, the noise of screams and shouts rose higher.

"Where will we go?" she asked.

"To the hills. Please, come on! Please, sister!"

Mouse looked at him suddenly. Sister . . .

"The hills?" she asked, half smiling.

"Let's go," Sigurd said, and took her hand.

They ran out and immediately were nearly killed. A horseman rode straight at them as soon as they appeared from the broch. But it was getting dark now, and the horseman missed his first deadly swing. Sigurd saw to it that it was his last, for he buried Fire-fresh in the man's ribs under his outstretched arm.

The Dark Horseman fell to the ground, instantly still. The horse reared above them.

"Come on!" yelled Sigurd, pulling Mouse away.

"No!" said Mouse. "Wait . . ."

She put a hand to the horse's side, and Sigurd watched amazed as it quickly calmed down, despite the noise all around. In a few more moments it stood peacefully, pushing its head into Mouse's hair.

"This way," she said, and without question Sigurd pushed her small body up onto the horse's shoulders, then swung himself into the saddle behind her.

And, to Sigurd's great shame, they ran away.

All around them the Storn ran crazily for cover. The dead lay thick between the brochs. As they fled Sigurd recognized Herda, a spear in his chest.

The invasion was almost over. Mouse and Sigurd rode on the invaders' horse out of the village. It was a powerful beast, and they hurtled away from the danger.

They could see the remains of their tribe running into the fields and, already beyond, reaching the foothills.

Here and there they could see someone being pursued by a Dark Horseman, and watched helplessly as he or she was put to the sword or spear.

"It's the end," wept Sigurd from the saddle. "This is the end."

Night fell as they escaped into the hills above what used to be their home.

19

We rode through the night. After a while I stopped trying to guide the horse and just let it pick its way through the lower slopes into the hills behind.

I had no idea where we were going, nor did I much care. If we had ridden into the Dark Horse camp, I think I would just have accepted it then. My attempt at being Lawspeaker was ill starred, and I could see no hope.

I thought Mouse was asleep, so I rested my head on her shoulder and closed my eyes.

I concentrated on the jogging of the horse and tried to block out the pain in my mind.

20

Mouse felt Sigurd put his head on her shoulder and guessed he might have fallen asleep.

The horse kept walking, and as the night grew deeper Mouse let herself into its mind. The horse obeyed and walked on up into the hills.

She lost track of time, but there was the faintest glow in the sky ahead of them. Dawn was not far away.

Without warning the horse stopped.

Mouse was surprised when Sigurd spoke.

"What is it, Mouse?"

"I don't know," she whispered back, then, "Wait. I think there's someone there. . . ."

Indeed there was. A shadow stepped out in front of them.

"Hold there!" said the shadow. "We have you outnumbered. Get down from the beast. . . ."

"I recognize that voice," said Sigurd. "Thorbjorn! Is that you?"

"Sigurd? Is that Mouse with you?"

They got down from the horse, and the three found one another in the darkness.

Despite everything, they laughed.

"Are you alone, Sigurd?" Thorbjorn asked.

"Yes, we . . ."

"It's all right, Sigurd. We all ran. There is no shame."

Sigurd shook his head in the dark. "So who else is here?"

"No one," said Thorbjorn quietly.

"So you had us outnumbered all by yourself?" asked Sigurd.

They laughed again.

"How did you get here so quickly? We've been traveling all night on the horse."

"Maybe so, but perhaps not as straight a path as I have taken—I climbed right up the cliff from the fields behind the village. Two hours' climb, maybe, and then I found myself here. I was too tired to go on, so I sat down to wait for the dawn, to see if I could find anyone else. . . . Then you came along. That's not Skinfax, is it?"

"No," said Sigurd, "I . . . we took it from one of the Dark Horse."

"Sigurd, you are indeed a brave warrior. I don't think we managed to put a stop to many of them."

"No," said Sigurd. It was his turn to be subdued. "What are we going to do?"

"Lawspeaker, I . . . ," Thorbjorn began, but he did not know what to say. Mouse spoke.

"We must find a place to sleep. I know a place."

"What?" said Sigurd. "How do you know a place?"

"I know," she said simply. "This is where I was born to you."

21

How we came to be there I could never understand, but it was all part of the path that fate had prepared for us. Much is clear now that was not then, if you understand that our lives are laid out for us and we merely follow the journey.

So we were back at the caves where we had found Mouse living with the wolves. That first night Mouse, Thorbjorn, and I crawled nervously inside the nearest one and got an hour or two's sleep while we waited for daylight.

"How do we know there aren't any wolves still here?" I had asked Mouse as she walked us calmly to the cave mouth.

"There aren't," she said. "They've all gone."

Something in her voice told me that what she was saying was true, could not be otherwise.

"Is this yours?" I asked Mouse.

"My what?" she answered.

"Your cave. Where you lived."

She shook her head.
"You don't understand," was all she said.
So we slept in a cave.

22

As daylight came and lit up the entrance of the cave Thorbjorn stirred. He got up and went to scout around outside. He was back very quickly.

"Sigurd! Mouse! Wake up! People coming."

They crept to the cave mouth, only to see Hemm, with his son Egil, leading a small group of the Storn up the slope toward them.

Sigurd stepped out to meet them.

"Hail!" he called from the top of the slope in front of the string of caves.

They embraced gladly for a few minutes but then grew quiet. They looked at one another.

Sigurd asked a question, though he was afraid of the answer.

"Have you seen Freya? Any of you?"

They all shook their heads.

"I told her to take Skinfax," he said.

But they looked back at him blankly.

"That's not necessarily bad," said Thorbjorn, putting a hand on his shoulder. "She could have got far away."

Sigurd nodded. It wouldn't do to show weakness. No doubt they each had lost someone when the Dark Horse attacked. It was up to him to lead the way.

But lead where? And to what end?

As the day wore on they took stock of their situation. They had a few swords and two spears. Otherwise, they had no food, nor water, nor any clothes apart from what they were standing in.

"All is lost!" wailed someone.

And Sigurd could not bring himself to disagree.

But then Mouse began to take over.

"I can help," she said. "For a start, I know where some others are hiding."

Sigurd turned to her. In spite of what he knew about her, he was surprised.

She held up a hand.

"There is a snake nearby. In the long grass by the cave mouth. It can smell humans. Upwind. That way."

And she pointed.

"How do we know they're not Dark Horse?"

"We don't, unless we go and look. Anyway, my guess is they'll all be in the village by now. . . ."

Sigurd could work again.

"Very well. Thorbjorn, Hemm, come with me. The rest

of you, I want you to find a water supply and anything we can eat. And if Mouse has any suggestions, follow her as you would me. . . ."

They left, Sigurd clutching Fire-fresh, Hemm and Thorbjorn with a sword and a spear between them.

23

It felt strange to be up on that bit of hillside again. It had been the best part of five years since we had found Mouse, and yet I recognized much of the landscape around us.

As Hemm and Thorbjorn and I went looking for more survivors of the attack, I remember worrying about the effect that being up on the hill might have on her. So far she seemed well, but she was so sensitive, I reasoned, that anything might happen.

It made me think of happier times, after Mouse had settled in with the Storn, before the famine had started—I was still a boy, a child, and Mouse was my little sister. We didn't have much work to do, and when it was done, we could spend the rest of the day wandering along the shore, swimming in the bay, or practicing hunting in the south woods.

But even then, I remember one time as we trailed each other through the woods she suddenly froze. As usual Mouse had found my hiding spot with great swiftness. She only had to ask the animals around her, and their feelings would give me away.

Laughing, I grabbed her and she squealed.

"Cheat!" I cried. "Try finding me yourself one day!"

And she was laughing but suddenly stopped. The look on her face made me let go of her straightaway.

"What is it?" I asked. I knew she was sensing something.

"Wolves," she said.

I must have looked scared, for she said, "No, not now. There were wolves here, but one died. Right here."

I don't know how she knew, but it had obviously upset her greatly. I took her home.

That's what I mean—she could sense something like that, and it could have a strong effect on her.

So I worried about what the caves might do to her. I was right to worry, as it turned out.

24

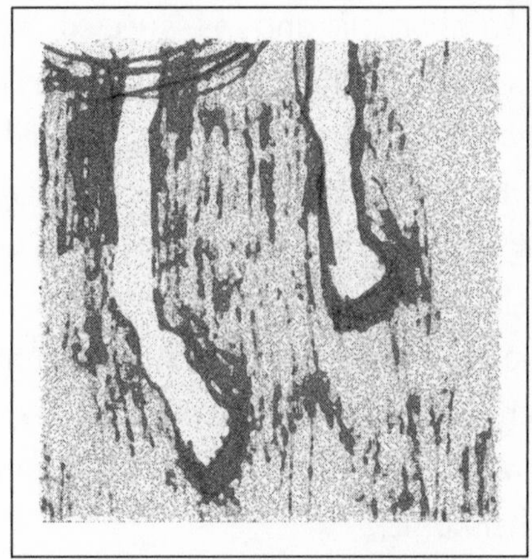

Sigurd and the others returned. They had found no one, but when they got back to the camp, more of the Storn were already there.

"They came around the top of the hill," Mouse explained, "as you were going to look for them along the side."

There were about sixteen of them now. The new arrivals included Hemm and Detlef, the Song-giver's son, who had seen his father killed in the attack.

Sigurd studied them all. They were quiet and looked at him hopefully, as if he was going to save them from all this mess.

"And there's something you must see," said Hemm. "Show him, Detlef."

Sigurd followed as the Song-maker's son took him back up onto the hills above the caves. It was a short but steep climb. They lay on a high spit of cliff, panting until their breath returned.

"Look," Detlef said, and pointed. Down, way down.

Incredibly, there was the village of the Storn, way below them. There was a sight line from high up on the cliff all the way down to the village. Even from this great height Sigurd could see individual buildings. The great broch was clearly visible, as was a weak, snaking column of smoke that rose out of what had been its roof. Other buildings were smoldering, too. The Dark Horse had destroyed the place.

"How are your eyes?" Sigurd asked Detlef.

"Yes, I see them, too," he said, understanding what Sigurd was asking.

There were figures walking around the village, and again, even at this distance, you could tell they were Dark Horse by their height and black garb.

"What are we going to do?" asked Detlef.

Sigurd wanted to tell the truth. Detlef was his own age, yet Sigurd already felt so much older. He could not let Detlef down.

"We'll survive," he said, but he felt he was lying. "Let's go down."

As Sigurd told the others what they had seen, that the Dark Horse, or at least some of them, were still in the village, the mood amongst them all grew blacker.

"We have water," said Mouse. "There's a stream a short way from here."

"And we have these," said one of the women, holding up a brace of hares. "We caught them," she explained needlessly.

Sigurd nodded.

"Good, now all we need is fire. We might just get some of this bracken to catch, but we're going to have to kindle it the old way. Who wants to try?"

Hemm volunteered. He got his small son Egil to help. It had been a long time since Hemm had lit a fire without flint and steel. They worked methodically, using the gut of one of the hares to make a string. They wound this once round a stick and then tied the ends to another stick. This made a bowstring, and when they ran it back and forth, the stick around which the gut was tied spun in a small hole in a third, flat piece of wood.

Eventually a little smoke began to drift from the hole, caused by the furious spinning of the bow stick.

"Try it," said Hemm, and Egil dropped a few crushed bits of dried bracken into the hole. He blew gently and a glow appeared. He repeated the process, and a small flame licked up the side of the bow stick.

"Quick!"

It was alight.

"Right," said Sigurd, "get the fire into the cave! We can't take the risk of being seen, even if we do need to eat."

Night was falling, the end of their first full day on the hill. They ate the hares, quietly and without joy. It had been a long time since anyone had asked Sigurd what they were going to do. He guessed that was because they knew he had no idea. There was only one person who didn't seem to feel the weight of sadness upon her.

Mouse.

25

Mouse had found the water. Mouse had sensed the presence of more of our tribe.

It was she who had told them where to look for the hares we ate. While the rest of us brooded over our own thoughts, Mouse seemed different.

A moment's reflection and I knew what it was. She was content.

We prepared to sleep. We had cut armfuls of bracken before dusk, using our swords. Now we passed as much of the stuff through the smoke of the fires as we could, in an effort to get rid of the ticks lurking in the bracken's fronds. It would be a restless night otherwise.

The ticks dropped from the bracken and crackled as they hit the fire. It would not get them all, but it might make the night a little more comfortable than the one before.

Then there was the problem with the horse. The invaders'

steed would not obey us. We needed to get it under cover, into the cave with us, but though the ceiling was high and there would be plenty of room for it to stand, it would not come inside.

I looked to Mouse for help, but she was uncooperative, too.

"Leave him outside," she said.

"No," I said. "We must get him inside. We can't take any chances."

Mouse looked at me. For a long time she said nothing but held my gaze. It suddenly occurred to me that we were having a fight, a battle of wills. I didn't know why, but it worried me.

"Mouse," I said quietly, "please get the horse to come in."

And finally she relented. She went and put her hand on its neck, and after a moment or two she was able to lead it into the cave. It snorted gently.

We gathered in the smoky darkness.

"Sigurd," someone said, "tonight is Spell-making. But we don't have Gudrun. . . ."

She was right. It was the full moon.

"Yes," said her sister. "What shall we do for Spell-making?"

It seemed obvious to me.

"Mouse," I said, "will you do the Spell-making for us?"

But again she refused, and this time I could not face forcing the issue. If she made me back down in front of the others, it would do me no good as leader, either.

"I cannot," she said, and that was all she would say. So I mumbled a few words to everyone and wished that we might yet prosper.

We slept. Or rather, some of us did, some of the time. Dawn was still a little way off as I rolled over on my bracken bed and saw that Mouse had gone. I thought she must have only just left, for I saw her moving out of the cave, a darker silhouette against a dark sky.

I got up and followed.

By the time I made it to the entrance, she was outside, farther along the series of cave mouths. She seemed to be heading somewhere, with purpose. It was clear she was not just sleepless and wandering aimlessly. Something about that made me want not to disturb her, but I followed, fascinated.

She made for a smaller cave, a little higher than the others, and went inside.

I hesitated, waiting for I do not know what. I looked out over the moonlit sea away beneath me, and I can clearly remember how beautiful it all seemed, despite the horror that had befallen us. There was not a cloud in the night sky, and the full moon shone as brightly as the sun at dawn.

I remembered Mouse. I climbed to the mouth of the cave. The moon was low in the sky now, and as I put my head up to look in, it illuminated the narrow, tunnel-like cave fully. Mouse was sitting at the back wall but was looking in, not out.

She seemed to be studying the wall. She was talking; it sounded as if she were talking to someone else, though there was no one there.

I decided she was not in any danger, and left her to her memories.

26

Next morning Sigurd sent Detlef and Mouse back up to the lookout point on the cliffs above them.

While they were gone, Sigurd spent some time organizing.

"For the time being, until we find the others, we are all that's left of the Storn," Sigurd said to the rest of the group.

They regarded him silently. There was no hostility, no disagreement, nor for that matter, agreement. There was nothing. Sigurd sensed that they had given up.

"Now is the time to prove ourselves. We need to relight the fire. And we need more wood so that we can keep it from going out again. We need to hunt for more food."

"Are we going to stay up here forever?" asked Hemm.

"Don't worry about that for now," said Sigurd a little desperately. "I'll work out what's best to do. . . ."

He bade them get on with their duties, before there were any more awkward questions.

He needed to think.

Should they look for the others? Should they return to the Storn itself? At least Detlef and Mouse might have some information that could help them decide.

Mouse.

What had she been doing last night? he wondered. He walked over to the cave where she had been. It wasn't hard to find. It was different from the others, smaller and higher up. Looking around to see that no one was watching, he went in. He paused for a moment, letting his eyes get used to the gloom inside.

After a while his vision became clearer, and he crawled toward the back of the low tunnel.

What had she been doing?

And then he saw it.

A drawing. And then another and another.

Bold drawings made with some dark brown stuff on the smooth back wall of the cave.

Sigurd did not understand them. The first thing he recognized was a picture of a wolf. He soon identified several more. Then there was something that looked like a huge, round tent. And then, as his eyes learned to understand what he was seeing, he saw some human figures. They were only stick drawings, but Sigurd could see a group of tall men dressed in heavy cloaks, and some women with arms raised. They pointed at the last, small figure.

"What are you doing here?" said Mouse, behind him.

"Nothing!" said Sigurd automatically. Then, remembering himself, he said, "Why? Should I not be here?"

"This is my place!" said Mouse.

Sigurd could not judge her mood. He crawled toward the opening, where his sister crouched.

"You mean when you lived with the wolves?"

Mouse ignored that question.

"What are these drawings?" Sigurd tried instead.

"How did you know they were here?" Mouse asked.

"I followed you last night," said Sigurd simply. "But how did *you* know about them?"

Mouse looked him straight in the eye.

"I made them," she said.

Sigurd couldn't help showing his surprise.

"You . . . ?" he began, but as so often before, he could tell the subject was closed. He left.

"Sorry," he said as he went, "I'm sorry. . . ."

He tried to hide it from Mouse, but his mind was racing, struck by a new terror. Again the girl he thought of as his sister had surprised him. They grew apart a little every time he realized how much he did not know about her. He had seen paintings on a wall in a long-forgotten cave, and she had told him they were hers.

Sigurd found that Detlef had returned, too, and was talking to the others.

"They've gone, Sigurd," said Thorbjorn as he approached.

"The Dark Horse?"

"Yes," said Detlef. "I couldn't see anyone down there at all. The fires are out, but there's still smoke."

"What about Mouse?" Sigurd asked.

"What do you mean?" replied Detlef.

"Could she . . . see anything? Feel anything?"

Detlef shook his head. "No. Nothing. They're gone."

A question lay unspoken in all their minds: Where?

Where had they gone?

Farther south, looking for more easy pickings?

Or had they gone back to the north, to their own lands?

Sigurd thought that was less likely. And there was another, more worrying possibility, too. Supposing they were coming to the hills? Coming to finish what they had started in the village?

Pictures and sounds from that terrifying night swept through Sigurd's mind again. So many of them! Dark brown and black cloaks swirling around their shoulders and white-haired heads as they swung sharp iron at anything that lay in their path. Unstoppable. And so many of the Storn dead.

They could not survive another attack. It would be the end of them all.

27

We did not see Mouse for most of the rest of that day. She spent a long time in her cave. I worried about what was happening to her. The rest of us argued.

We argued about what the disappearance of the Dark Horse meant, whether it was a good or a bad sign. We argued about what we should do either way.

Some of the tribe wanted to go back to the village. Others said that was certain death. I was rapidly losing control; I was on the edge of losing my status entirely, because they could tell I was struggling.

And then, late in the afternoon, as we sat around the fire in the cave, Mouse appeared at the entrance. The horse whinnied as he saw her.

"I have seen the Dark Horse," Mouse said. "They are coming for us."

And that changed everything.

28

The difference between them spoke much in itself. The small foundling girl, back on her hillside, stood and spoke calmly but urgently about what she had seen. The rest of the Storn, or what was left of them, stood in a ragged bunch, weak, dispirited, and defeated. Even Sigurd's proud young heart was failing him.

And so Mouse took charge.

"In the mind of a wolf I ran down to the Dark Horse. They are camped in the low hills. At least they were."

"Where are they now?" asked Sigurd. He could feel his heart starting to beat stronger and faster. He looked desperately at Mouse, too scared to marvel at the change in her.

"All is clear," said Mouse. "They have again divided into two groups."

At this news, which indicated another attack, there were shouts and cries. Of fear, of pain.

"There is only one chance," said Mouse firmly. "There is

a narrow gully that runs inland. It is not far from here. Detlef and I saw it when we went to look for the others. I have felt my way along. It opens into a wooded valley."

Sigurd nodded, understanding Mouse's plan.

"From there we can hide in the woods," he said. "And move through them far away until the Dark Horse give up."

He tried to sound more confident than he felt. Would the Dark Horse ever give up? If they would follow the Storn once, why would they ever stop? But at least it was a plan; it was a chance of survival for the tribe.

There was still no sign of any of the others, of his mother. Sigurd shook himself.

"Right," he said. "We leave. Now!"

And there were no arguments.

They got their few possessions together and followed Mouse out of the camp.

Sigurd thought Mouse might refuse to leave the caves, or at least find it hard to do so, but he was wrong.

She led them away from her old home and didn't look back.

29

Sigurd brought up the rear, leading the horse by its leather bridle. Horse and boy surveyed the group in front of them—the last of the Storn, for all they knew. All were quiet.

Mouse had taken command of their situation and was leading them to safety, toward the gully that would take them to the forests inland. And Sigurd admitted to himself that he did not mind. To be Lawspeaker was hard enough; to be Lawspeaker at a time of war, even harder. With only a touch of guilt he gladly let Mouse help them for a while. It was *her* plan and a good one—once inside the trees they would stand a much better chance of getting right away from the Dark Horse. Random, bloody images from the attack flashed like a sword through his memory again. He shuddered.

"Come on," called Mouse from the front. "Quickly! Don't lag behind!"

She was right. The Storn had straggled out into a line. Now gaps were appearing.

"Come on," she said again, more urgently. For the first time in a long time she looked to Sigurd for support. "Tell them, Sigurd."

Sigurd shook himself.

"Yes," he said. "Yes, we must hurry now. Our only chance is to make it to the woods!"

They moved on again and made better progress toward the top of the gully that Detlef and Mouse had seen. The landscape round them had changed. They could no longer see the sea. That itself was unusual for the Storn, whose lives were dominated by the sight and sound and smell of the ocean, whose lives up until a few days ago had depended on it.

They were walking over rolling ground high up behind the hills where the caves were. After an hour or so the landscape began to change. The ground grew into hills around them, until the slopes had become unclimbable rock faces on either side of them. Almost without realizing it, they were in the gully. Something about it was oppressive, intimidating.

"Mouse," called Sigurd. "How long is the journey to the forests from here?"

She didn't look round from her position at the front.

"Mouse!" he called again, an edge in his voice this time.

"A bird's flight," she called back, but without looking round.

One or two of the others looked at Sigurd, unspoken questions on their lips.

He nodded.

"Then we had better hurry," he said.

30

As we entered the gully I felt a shadow closing in. A warning to my soul. But I did not heed it, and it was not long before we found ourselves deep in the throat of the mountains.

With each step the hills on either side of us grew higher and more impassable.

We could only go forward or back.

We could only hope that the Dark Horse did not have our trail.

Mouse still led the way. Behind her walked Thorbjorn, my father's closest ally, still serving the Storn well by carrying more than his share. I was still at the back, leading the horse, which made light of the load on its back.

The horse! I should have heeded it, too, though by then it was too late.

We had been in the gully for an hour when suddenly the beast spooked. It snorted loudly and threw its head in the air, trying to pull the bridle from my hands. Nostrils flaring, it let out a loud whinny.

Then it stopped dead and refused to move at all.

I tugged hard at its bridle, but there was no way I could move it against its will.

"Mouse!" I called to the front. "Can you . . . ?"

But she was already coming back down the line.

She didn't look at me but calmly took the horse's bridle and pulled its head down to hers. I swear that she spoke to it. I swear that she whispered in its ear and that it then moved on happily.

She took it up to the front of the line, but no sooner had they got there than it stopped again and reared into the air, standing high on its back legs. It let out the loudest call I ever heard it make, and then it sank back to the ground.

And in the silence that followed, as we stood, spooked ourselves by now, there came an answer to the horse's call. The cry of another horse came to us.

I have told you this story, this whole story, of Mouse and me, as best I can. At times my memory has failed me, and I have not been able to remember everything that I should have. But I remember every single moment of what happened that day. It is burned into my memory, branded there by pain.

I remember it all, but I cannot talk about it with ease.

The Dark Horse came upon us.

Without further warning than that horse's cry, they came sweeping up the gully in front of us. Out of nowhere they were there—their terrible black cloaks swinging from their shoulders as they galloped toward us.

We stood frozen, unable to do anything. We prepared to die. Suddenly there came a terrible shriek from the oncoming horsemen.

I knew what it meant, for it was answered from behind. We

whirled around and saw the other half of the Dark Horse coming at us from behind. They had us trapped, just as they had when they destroyed Storn.

As they approached I drew Fire-fresh from my side. I was still at the back. Hemm was beside me with a spear.

I looked desperately to the front, to Mouse, and realized the horsemen would get *there* first. I started to run toward her.

The first horseman was almost there. I would not make it, but Thorbjorn stepped forward, in front of Mouse, sword in hand.

The horseman met him, and as Thorbjorn raised his arm to strike he received a spear through his chest. He was dead before he hit the ground.

And then.

And then.

And then, this is the part I struggle to tell you.

The horseman reached Mouse.

She put her arms out in front of her, raised them slightly above her head. And the horseman leaned down in his saddle and grabbed her outstretched arms and swung her up into the saddle in front of him.

Everything stopped. The horsemen surrounded us, but no more blows were struck. They all gazed at Mouse, who with the help of the rider stood on the horse's back.

And then the Dark Horse let out the loudest shout of all.

"Kara!" they cried as one. "Kara! Kara! Kara!"

And Mouse stood on the horse, waving at them. She was smiling.

"Kara! Kara! Kara!"

31

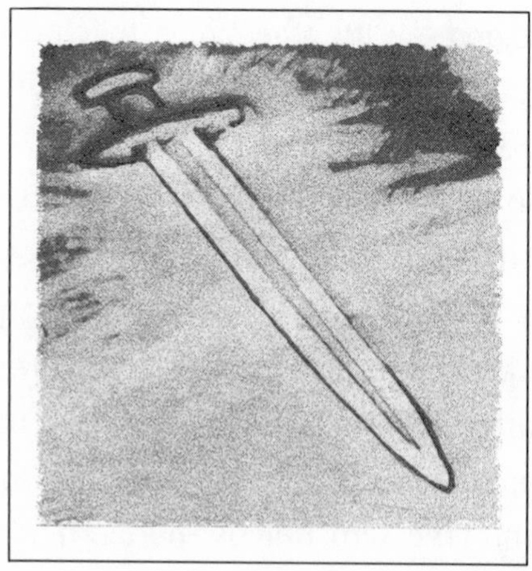

Sigurd sat by himself in one of the cages, Hemm in another next to him. Two more were hunched up in a third; all the others sat silently in their own little prisons in ones and twos. The cages were small boxes made of posts lashed together with leather ropes. They were tiny, and it was impossible to sit up straight in them, let alone stand.

The only one missing was Thorbjorn, whose body still lay up in the gully where he had fallen.

Wrong. There was one other missing. Mouse.

Betrayed.

The Storn were too shocked to speak. Too shocked even to wonder why they had not been killed already. The Dark Horse had spared no one during their first attack, but no one even cared to think why this time should be any different.

They had been led into the gully. By Mouse, who had known just where she was taking them. And they had walked right into the trap.

Sigurd stared out of his cage at the world around him, with his heart broken and mind bent in equal measure.

Once the Storn had been captured, their hands had been tied and they had been slung across the backs of the horses. The whole journey had become a waking nightmare for Sigurd. He was still struggling to take in what had happened. He hadn't seen Mouse since she had stood on the back of the horse. The Dark Horse had called out—they had called out for Mouse, that was clear, but what had they called her? Kara? Sigurd struggled to make sense of it but could not.

The Dark Horse had taken them on down through the gully. After a long time they had finally reached its end.

There, just beyond a small patch of heath, lay the woods for which they had been heading.

The forest had been their chance to survive, but as the horse on which he was being carried turned and came to a halt, Sigurd saw something on the open ground in front of the trees.

The Dark Horse's encampment. A dozen—maybe more—huge, round domed tents covered the ground. Each was taller than two men at its center and was perhaps fifty paces round. Horses stood tethered amongst the tents; people came and went. Smoke came from the vent in the center of each tent's roof, and for some strange reason there were fires burning on the grass outside the camp, too.

Sigurd had felt a tear roll down his face as he bounced and bumped the last few yards on the horse's back.

Then he and the others had been dragged roughly from

their mounts and thrown into the small wooden cages, where they had passed the rest of the day. The cages stood a little away from the outermost of the tents, and from there the last of the Storn had been able to watch the Dark Horse going about their business. For the first time Sigurd could see that they were just people, not monsters. All the Storn had seen of them until then were galloping horses and flashing swords, but now he could watch the whole tribe. He saw their women carrying supplies, food and wood and water, to and fro. They were making preparations for a feast. He saw the men, still terrifyingly huge but engaged in mundane tasks. Chopping wood, tending horses.

Then he saw Mouse standing in front of his cage.

She had approached quietly while he had been staring at the tents in front of him.

She looked at him. The others looked away, though someone spat at her through the bars of his cage. Sigurd felt the same way, except he wanted to do worse than that. Stuck inside his cage, he could do nothing but glare at her.

"Try and understand," Mouse said, looking at him steadily. Her voice was calm, and cool.

Sigurd nearly laughed at her. His mind was twisting under the pressure to understand what had happened to them.

"Understand!" he yelled at Mouse. "Understand?"

In a few short days the Storn had been reduced to a handful of prisoners in cages. Ragnald had come and brought death to his father and to Sif's. Then the Dark Horse had come to finish the job.

"What have you done to us?" cried Sigurd. "We are

your family! They came and destroyed us once! Then you finish us!"

"No, Sigurd," said Mouse. "You finished yourselves. You are useless. The Storn have nothing. No skills, no fight, no warriors, no one to use magic. You are nothing, you have come to nothing."

Sigurd fought again to understand. Again he could not.

"But why?" he cried. "Why? How can you betray us? We are your family! I am your brother."

"No," said Mouse. "You are not my brother. You are not my family."

She waved an arm at the encampment behind her. "*This* is my family."

32

Slowly Sigurd began to understand.

"This is my family. My true family. Where I was born. Where I lived before I lived with the wolves."

That was what Mouse told him.

Then one of the Dark Horse came to fetch her. He towered above her. Clearly he did not like the idea of her talking to the captives, but when he spoke to her, it was with respect, as if she was the more powerful.

"Come," he said. "Come away now. There is much to be done. Ketil wants to talk to you."

He shot a look at Sigurd that made his stomach sicken with fear.

Mouse looked up at the warrior.

"Yes, Ulf," she said. "Tell Ketil I am coming."

The warrior, Ulf, nodded and left.

"I must go now, Sigurd," she said.

"What about us?" shouted Hemm.

Some of the others shouted abuse at her.

She turned to go.

"What about us?" cried Sigurd. "How can you do this to us?"

"You are not dead," said Mouse, but that was all.

"Princess!" called Ulf from the edge of the tents. He had seen that Mouse was still talking to Sigurd.

"Ulf!" she called back, and walked away.

Princess? thought Sigurd. Princess?

How could she be their princess? This was Mouse. This was his *sister.* Or had been for a few short years. And now he was to accept that she had betrayed them, had led them to their end, in hutches.

"Sigurd," said Hemm from the cage next to his. "Sigurd!"

Sigurd ignored him.

"Sigurd Olafsson!" called Hemm again.

Sigurd looked up.

"What are we going to do?" Hemm asked.

Sigurd shook his head. "I don't know."

"Is that it?" Hemm shouted. "You lead us to our death, and then . . . and then what?"

"I didn't lead you. . . ."

"No, it was that treacherous bitch! Your sister!"

Sigurd looked away. He let his head rest against the bars of the cage and wished for it all to end.

"It seems she is still a wolf after all! There is no good in her, though we tried to make her one of us!"

And though he said nothing, Sigurd could not help agreeing.

33

It was getting dark. Sigurd hadn't spoken a word since Mouse had left. He sat hunched up in his cage, listening to one of his people sobbing. He had failed them all, not just the few left rotting in the cages, but the others, too. Thorbjorn. The others who had died in the first attack. Even Sif had deserved better. He thought about his mother, and he cried more silent tears.

Sigurd had failed them all, but what was worse was that he had given up. All that filled his mind was Mouse and what she had done.

He saw someone coming over to them from the tents. The tallest horseman he had seen so far. He strode over to the cages and walked up and down, looking at each in turn.

"Who is Sigurd?" he said when he had studied them all.

No one said anything, but the man seemed to have worked it out himself.

He came over and stood in front of Sigurd's cage.

"You are Sigurd, called Lawspeaker?" he asked. His accent was thick and strange, but Sigurd understood him well enough.

"I am Sigurd Olafsson, Lawspeaker of the Storn," said Sigurd with as much courage as he could muster.

"Very well," said the man, "I am Ketil, and these are my people. We are happy today because our long search is over. We have been reunited with our princess, Kara. Tonight we will celebrate. But there is something first."

Sigurd detected a threatening note in Ketil's voice.

"Kara has asked that we spare your lives. I have accepted her wishes, since she is our princess."

"Then what will happen to us?" asked Hemm.

"Do your people normally insult their Lawspeaker in this way?" Ketil asked Sigurd.

Sigurd looked at Hemm.

"He has a right to speak," said Sigurd. "He wants to know what will happen to us. And I do, too."

"You belong to us now. In return for your lives you will serve us, until you die."

"Be your slaves?" asked Sigurd. He stared at Ketil for a long time, but the man did not so much as twitch. "And if we refuse?"

"Then you will be put to death."

The Storn held their breath. They watched their boy leader intently. Their fate hung by a thread.

"So, you will be ours," Ketil said, and turned to leave, a smirk on his face.

"No," said Sigurd.

Ketil stopped and looked at Sigurd.

"No?" he said.

But Sigurd ignored him. He turned to his people.

"People of Storn, listen to me, your Lawspeaker, for the last time. I have led you badly. I could not protect you from the famine, nor from these people. We have been scattered and destroyed, and the tribe may soon be extinct. But I would rather it was extinct than that it survived, half alive, as slaves to these killers."

Ketil watched with interest as he spoke but made no effort to stop him.

"And so, hear my last words as Lawspeaker. I end my life as Lawspeaker. I end the life of the tribe. The Storn are no more, but they will never be slaves. You are free to choose your own destiny, but I for one will go to my death proudly."

He stopped and stared at his kin. They looked at him with a mixture of fear and wonder on their faces. There was absolute silence, and then someone spoke.

"I go with you, Lawspeaker."

Detlef, the Song-giver's son.

"I go with Sigurd," he said again. "My father is gone, his music is dead. I want nothing more. Let the tribe die with pride."

Silent looks passed between the Storn.

And then they all pointed at Sigurd.

"We go with our Lawspeaker," they said.

34

Strange.

For in that moment, the moment in which I believed that all was lost, that there was nothing left—no hope, nor fear, nor joy, nor pain—something came to me.

Pride. And as each of my people decided to die, with me, our pride grew stronger. And as it grew stronger it became something else—it became strength. And as Ketil cursed us all and strode away it became something even greater—power.

I realized I had been wrong. There *was* hope after all.

Ketil walked back to the tents, and as he did so Detlef began to sing one of his father's favorite songs. It was a joyful song we all knew well, and we joined in, and though we still faced death, I believe it was at that moment that we were reborn.

35

Mouse. Kara. Whoever she was, she had heard about the decision the Storn had made. She came straight to Sigurd, who fell silent. The others did not cease their singing, but if anything, sang with more heart than ever. They wanted to show her that they had something after all.

"Why, Sigurd, why?" she said. "You are choosing to die!"

Sigurd could not judge her mood. He did not trust her anymore. He had been wrong about who she was all these years. He could not judge her intentions, nor her thoughts. Why did she care now whether they lived or died?

"What life will it be to act as slaves," he asked, "to these animals!"

That made her angry. "They are not animals!"

"No," said Sigurd. "Even a wolf could not be so vicious."

That stopped her. She fought with thoughts in her head.

"They are my people," she said at last. "I belong with them just as you belong to the Storn."

"And do you owe the Storn nothing? The people who took you in, who rescued you from wolves?"

"I never wanted rescuing!" she shouted. "You took me from them! You burnt us and killed us and took me away!"

Sigurd looked at the stranger in front of him.

"Who are you? How did you ever live with wolves if these are your people?"

Mouse grew quieter again. She seemed to be weighing up what she would tell Sigurd.

"I was born to these people, whom you call Dark Horse. That is not our own name. I am their princess. Ketil is my father's brother and leads the tribe now. When I was still a small child, I was abducted by a band of outlaws. They fled with me, intending to claim ransom, but they were in turn attacked by another tribe. I was taken by that tribe, a year passed, maybe more, but one day I escaped. I was far from home, very far, and I did not know where I was. I wandered through hills for many months. And then I found the wolves. Or they found me. I do not know why, but they found me sleeping wild on the hill and treated me as one of their own kind. They raised me.

"Then began my time of forgetting. All that I have just told you was not known to me anymore."

"Then how . . . ?" began Sigurd.

"How do I know all this? The tribe had not given me up entirely. At least, they began to believe I might be alive, because of Ulf. The one you saw earlier. He is our wise man. He felt my presence in a dream.

"So they began to search for me. They sent a man."

"Ragnald?"

"And with him the box..."

She paused.

"What was it?" asked Sigurd.

"A box of memories. My memories."

"But if you remembered everything, then why did you run away with us to the hills?"

"The box was strong magic, but it was only a start. Things began to come back. Who I was... Then in the cave..."

"The drawings? Your drawings?"

"Yes. I made those drawings when I was new to the wolf caves, before I forgot everything," she said. "The wolf father was attacked by a young male. They were fighting for control of the pack. Just like Olaf and Horn. The older wolf lost. I made the drawings with his blood, to try and remember what had happened to me. When I saw them again, I remembered the tents and the horses and the cold wind of the dark lands to the north where we used to ride. It all came back to me."

Memories drawn in blood.

Sigurd was silent.

"So I had to find them," she said.

"But you didn't have to betray us," said Sigurd.

Mouse said nothing.

"Your people are killers, Mouse. Look at what they did to us! How can you live with them?"

But she did not get the chance to answer, because suddenly two of the Dark Horse found her.

"Inside," one of them said. "You are missed."

He spoke briskly, obviously uneasy that their princess was speaking to the prisoners.

"Sigurd . . . ," said Mouse, but they led her away.

Night fell. The Dark Horse began their feasting.

36

We sat in the darkness. It was a cold night, but we had been given no fire to keep us warm. No one slept, and not just because of the cold. It's hard to sleep when you know you will die in the morning.

"Did I do the right thing?" I wondered. I didn't realize I'd said it aloud until Hemm answered me.

"Yes, Lawspeaker," he said. "If only we'd shown this courage a little earlier."

"When they attacked the first time?" I asked.

"No," he said. "Months ago, maybe years . . . we lost our way with Horn. . . ."

We fell silent again. Then from out of my mind came words I had spoken. Words that, when spoken, had been about Ragnald, but that now had a more bitter meaning.

"Have we had one of the Dark Horse in our midst and not realized it?"

. . .

Detlef sang another song for us. He chose a sad song, a lament that was sung in honor of fallen heroes. I thought about Thorbjorn again. He was truly a man worth remembering. Faithful and honest.

Detlef sang on.

And then, in the darkness, there came a voice.

"Why sing sad songs?" it said. "We are not yet dead."

I turned as well as I could in the cramped cage and peered into the darkness.

"Who's there?" I whispered. The voice had come from the side of the cages that faced the forest.

"It's me," said the voice.

Then I recognized it.

"Sif?" I gasped.

"Yes, and Grinling and Bran. There are many of us."

Too many questions struggled to be the first to my lips.

"Why?" was the one I asked, stupidly, for it was the one I already knew the answer to.

"To save the Storn," she said.

I was aware then of others creeping quietly up to the cages. Dimly I saw the glint of a sword.

"How many are we?" I asked.

"I have twenty warriors here. The weak and the injured are in hiding in the forest. We have Gudrun! She is caring for them. Your mother is there, too, Sigurd."

"Freya!" I cried.

I could feel my strength awakening.

"I wish we were more," said Sif, "but we have some weapons."

"They are drunk and fattened," I told her. "There is no better chance for us. Get us out!"

"Yes, Lawspeaker," she said.

I could have laughed.

37

The Storn fell upon the Dark Horse with no warning and no mercy. They knew their only chance was to take the Dark Horse by surprise, before they could ready themselves.

Sif and Sigurd crawled on their bellies to the edge of the outermost tent, directing their small army to spread out around them. The Dark Horse had no guards posted, so confident of their power that they never expected to be attacked.

"There!" said Sif. "Look!"

She pointed through the maze of tents to the center of the camp. There stood the equivalent of the Storn's own great broch—a mighty domed structure of skins, ropes, and poles that blotted out the night sky behind it like a mountain. From inside came the bulk of the noise and the light.

"What do we do?" asked Sif.

Sigurd looked at her.

"Don't you hate me anymore?" he asked.

She pulled the neck of her tunic down and showed Sigurd the scar that had formed where she had been burnt.

"Do you have one of these?" she asked.

Sigurd understood her. Their world had changed, but Sif and Sigurd had become the same.

"Then let's show them why stone houses are safer than ones made of skin!" he said.

Sif looked puzzled, but Sigurd twanged the rope of the tent that they lay next to.

"Give me your dagger," he said, grinning in the moonlight.

Sigurd, Sif, Detlef, Hemm, and his son Egil each cut the allotted rope at the same time. The effect was just what they had hoped. The vast tent fell in on itself immediately, and almost as soon as it fell, it was alight with the fire that had been in its center.

Figures struggled out and were cut down by the Storn as they emerged. For a short time it looked as if there would be no battle at all. But now the alarm was raised, and other tents spewed out Dark Horse, who, despite being drunk, began to deal their terrible blows around them.

Still, though, the Storn had the upper hand. Other tents had been sliced down and set alight now, and the heath had become one big bonfire in the night.

"Come on!" Sif cried with renewed belief, and led them forward to finish the Dark Horse. They all followed, all except Sigurd, whose eyes were elsewhere.

Away to the side, in the shadow of one of the few tents still standing, crouched Mouse.

"Mouse!" he shouted. "Mouse!"

She heard him and jumped to her feet.

"Come here!" he shouted, but she did just the opposite. Like a hunted wolf, she bolted out of the ring of fire and made off into the darkness. Sigurd took one look at the fight, which was near to closing, and sped after her.

He caught sight of her just before she leaped out of the camp entirely and headed for the woods. She ran as an animal does, holding nothing back. Sigurd did the same.

Mouse had the advantage, Sigurd knew that. Her eyes were sharp in the dark.

Like a wolf, he thought.

But there she was, just at the edge of the trees. Once inside, in the dark, it would be harder to find her, almost impossible. He pulled an extra burst of speed from his burning legs and dove into the forest after her.

He could hear her just ahead, scuttling through undergrowth, and then, suddenly, silence.

He pounded on for a few steps and then he fell. Over Mouse.

"Sigurd!" she cried.

Sigurd rolled to his feet and grabbed her legs as she tried to get up.

"No, Sigurd!" she cried. "Let me go."

But Sigurd pushed her back to the ground and sat on her before she could slip away into the darkness.

He drew the dagger Sif had given him and raised it above Mouse's head.

"No, Sigurd, no!" she cried again.

His hand hovered.

"You said I was your sister!"

"I know," he screamed back. His hand shook. "And look how you repay me!" he shouted.

"No, please!"

Sigurd's hand rose a little higher, anger flooded through him. She had betrayed them. She had caused some of them to die. She had killed her own family. She! The little Mouse who had begged him to be her brother!

He plunged the dagger downward and thrust it into the earth beside her head, crying.

For a while they held each other, crying tears into each other's clothes. The sounds of the fight from the Dark Horse's camp had subsided. It was over. Between the trees they could see the skins of the tents burning like gigantic torches in the night.

"Are you going to let me live?" asked Mouse between sobs.

"How can I kill you? I promised to be your brother. I cannot kill you."

"I'm sorry, Sigurd," cried Mouse. She wailed and wailed. "I'm sorry for what I have done! But I belong with them!"

Sigurd shook his head.

Mouse crawled away from him.

"What am I going to do?" she cried.

"You cannot stay here. You are no longer one of the Storn!"

"But you let me live! That means you forgive me?"

"I let you live," said Sigurd, "but I cannot answer for the others, Lawspeaker or not."

He did not answer her other question.

"Then there is nothing for me."

Sigurd got to his feet wearily.

"No," he said, "there is nothing. Or maybe nothing itself is something."

Mouse quieted a little as she began to understand what he meant.

"You have betrayed your foster family. They, in turn, have destroyed the tribe you were born to. You have no home now. But I think you were happiest when you had no home at all."

Mouse stood up, too.

She was quiet but shook a little. Tears dropped from her eyes.

"Yes," she said.

Sigurd raised his hand slowly. Gently he wiped the tears from Mouse's eyes.

"Yes," said Mouse again, "I understand."

She stepped forward and held Sigurd's hands in hers.

"Sigurd?" she asked.

He knew what she was asking.

"Yes," he said. "I will always be your brother."

There was a long silence between them. Mouse let Sigurd's hands fall free from her own, and then she spoke for the last time.

“Keep my memories for me,” she said. “When you find them.”

Sigurd shook his head, confused. He looked at her, a question on his lips, but Mouse said nothing more.

She turned and, without looking back, walked into the depths of the forest.

Epilogue

When I returned to the camp, it was all over. My people had found courage and had fought bravely, and we had prevailed.

From out of the woods the rest of the tribe emerged. And there was my mother.

Stupid! Even old as I am now, with Freya long in the ground, tears prick my eyes at the thought of that reunion.

So we survived, and more than that. We rebuilt our village by the sea, and Sif and I, as husband and wife, pulled the Storn through famine until better times came again. And Gudrun, who had somehow foreseen this union, was our Wisewoman for many years. I asked her once what game she had been playing the night she had Sif and me carry her into the great broch. She said it had been her plan that Sif and I should marry. She had seen what no one else had, that the warring between our fathers could have been ended this way. But there was something more, she said.

"Love is often hidden to those lost in it."

"But Sif hated me then!" I protested.

"No, she was just jealous."

Of me and Mouse, Gudrun meant.

Gudrun grew to be a very old woman, kept healthy, I believe, by her herbs and potions.

. . .

And Mouse?

I told the Storn that she had died in the fight, and no one dared to ask me if that was really true, or to ask to see her body. And though I hadn't understood her last words to me at the time, it wasn't long before their meaning was revealed. As we struggled during that first winter we ate our way through the pile of grain in the barn where Ragnald had died. And one day, as the mound grew yet smaller, the box of memories appeared from where it had been hidden, I guessed, by Mouse.

So I keep her memories for her, the memories of who she truly was, though who she truly was is something I do not like to think of.

And the years have come and gone, and I think about my life, and I realize that many of my own memories are memories of blood.

From time to time traders come and go, and sometimes they tell stories. We gather round the fire in the great broch to listen, and sometimes the stories tell of a figure seen in the woods.

It is said to be a spirit, or a phantom, or even a woman, who walks through the woods with wolves at her heels.

And as I hear these stories I smile.

MARCUS SEDGWICK was a sales manager for a children's publisher in England and now works as an editor for a children's book packager. He is the author of *Witch Hill,* which was nominated for an Edgar Award for Best Young Adult Mystery, and *Floodland,* which was hailed as a "dazzling debut" and won the Branford Boase Award for best first novel.

Marcus Sedgwick grew up in East Kent and graduated from the University of Bath. In addition to writing, he does stone carvings, etchings, and woodcuts. He has a five-year-old daughter.